JUST OUTSIDE

(A Cami Lark Mystery —Book Two)

BLAKE PIERCE

Blake Pierce

Blake Pierce is the USA Today bestselling author of the RILEY PAGE mystery series, which includes seventeen books. Blake Pierce is also the author of the MACKENZIE WHITE mystery series, comprising fourteen books; of the AVERY BLACK mystery series, comprising six books; of the KERI LOCKE mystery series, comprising five books; of the MAKING OF RILEY PAIGE mystery series, comprising six books; of the KATE WISE mystery series, comprising seven books; of the CHLOE FINE psychological suspense mystery, comprising six books; of the JESSIE HUNT psychological suspense thriller series, comprising twenty six books; of the AU PAIR psychological suspense thriller series, comprising three books; of the ZOE PRIME mystery series, comprising six books; of the ADELE SHARP mystery series, comprising sixteen books, of the EUROPEAN VOYAGE cozy mystery series, comprising six books; of the LAURA FROST FBI suspense thriller, comprising eleven books; of the ELLA DARK FBI suspense thriller, comprising fourteen books (and counting); of the A YEAR IN EUROPE cozy mystery series, comprising nine books, of the AVA GOLD mystery series, comprising six books; of the RACHEL GIFT mystery series, comprising ten books (and counting); of the VALERIE LAW mystery series, comprising nine books (and counting); of the PAIGE KING mystery series, comprising eight books (and counting); of the MAY MOORE mystery series, comprising eleven books (and counting); the CORA SHIELDS mystery series, comprising five books (and counting); of the NICKY LYONS mystery series, comprising seven books (and counting), of the CAMI LARK mystery series, comprising five books (and counting), and of the new AMBER YOUNG mystery series, comprising five books (and counting).

An avid reader and lifelong fan of the mystery and thriller genres, Blake loves to hear from you, so please feel free to visit www.blakepierceauthor.com to learn more and stay in touch.

ISBN: 978-1-0943-8039-1

BOOKS BY BLAKE PIERCE

AMBER YOUNG MYSTERY SERIES
ABSENT PITY (Book #1)
ABSENT REMORSE (Book #2)
ABSENT FEELING (Book #3)
ABSENT MERCY (Book #4)
ABSENT REASON (Book #5)

CAMI LARK MYSTERY SERIES
JUST ME (Book #1)
JUST OUTSIDE (Book #2)
JUST RIGHT (Book #3)
JUST FORGET (Book #4)
JUST ONCE (Book #5)

NICKY LYONS MYSTERY SERIES
ALL MINE (Book #1)
ALL HIS (Book #2)
ALL HE SEES (Book #3)
ALL ALONE (Book #4)
ALL FOR ONE (Book #5)
ALL HE TAKES (Book #6)
ALL FOR ME (Book #7)

CORA SHIELDS MYSTERY SERIES
UNDONE (Book #1)
UNWANTED (Book #2)
UNHINGED (Book #3)
UNSAID (Book #4)
UNGLUED (Book #5)

MAY MOORE SUSPENSE THRILLER
NEVER RUN (Book #1)
NEVER TELL (Book #2)
NEVER LIVE (Book #3)
NEVER HIDE (Book #4)
NEVER FORGIVE (Book #5)

NEVER AGAIN (Book #6)
NEVER LOOK BACK (Book #7)
NEVER FORGET (Book #8)
NEVER LET GO (Book #9)
NEVER PRETEND (Book #10)
NEVER HESITATE (Book #11)

PAIGE KING MYSTERY SERIES
THE GIRL HE PINED (Book #1)
THE GIRL HE CHOSE (Book #2)
THE GIRL HE TOOK (Book #3)
THE GIRL HE WISHED (Book #4)
THE GIRL HE CROWNED (Book #5)
THE GIRL HE WATCHED (Book #6)
THE GIRL HE WANTED (Book #7)
THE GIRL HE CLAIMED (Book #8)

VALERIE LAW MYSTERY SERIES
NO MERCY (Book #1)
NO PITY (Book #2)
NO FEAR (Book #3)
NO SLEEP (Book #4)
NO QUARTER (Book #5)
NO CHANCE (Book #6)
NO REFUGE (Book #7)
NO GRACE (Book #8)
NO ESCAPE (Book #9)

RACHEL GIFT MYSTERY SERIES
HER LAST WISH (Book #1)
HER LAST CHANCE (Book #2)
HER LAST HOPE (Book #3)
HER LAST FEAR (Book #4)
HER LAST CHOICE (Book #5)
HER LAST BREATH (Book #6)
HER LAST MISTAKE (Book #7)
HER LAST DESIRE (Book #8)
HER LAST REGRET (Book #9)
HER LAST HOUR (Book #10)

AVA GOLD MYSTERY SERIES

CITY OF PREY (Book #1)
CITY OF FEAR (Book #2)
CITY OF BONES (Book #3)
CITY OF GHOSTS (Book #4)
CITY OF DEATH (Book #5)
CITY OF VICE (Book #6)

A YEAR IN EUROPE
A MURDER IN PARIS (Book #1)
DEATH IN FLORENCE (Book #2)
VENGEANCE IN VIENNA (Book #3)
A FATALITY IN SPAIN (Book #4)

ELLA DARK FBI SUSPENSE THRILLER
GIRL, ALONE (Book #1)
GIRL, TAKEN (Book #2)
GIRL, HUNTED (Book #3)
GIRL, SILENCED (Book #4)
GIRL, VANISHED (Book 5)
GIRL ERASED (Book #6)
GIRL, FORSAKEN (Book #7)
GIRL, TRAPPED (Book #8)
GIRL, EXPENDABLE (Book #9)
GIRL, ESCAPED (Book #10)
GIRL, HIS (Book #11)
GIRL, LURED (Book #12)
GIRL, MISSING (Book #13)
GIRL, UNKNOWN (Book #14)

LAURA FROST FBI SUSPENSE THRILLER
ALREADY GONE (Book #1)
ALREADY SEEN (Book #2)
ALREADY TRAPPED (Book #3)
ALREADY MISSING (Book #4)
ALREADY DEAD (Book #5)
ALREADY TAKEN (Book #6)
ALREADY CHOSEN (Book #7)
ALREADY LOST (Book #8)
ALREADY HIS (Book #9)
ALREADY LURED (Book #10)
ALREADY COLD (Book #11)

EUROPEAN VOYAGE COZY MYSTERY SERIES
MURDER (AND BAKLAVA) (Book #1)
DEATH (AND APPLE STRUDEL) (Book #2)
CRIME (AND LAGER) (Book #3)
MISFORTUNE (AND GOUDA) (Book #4)
CALAMITY (AND A DANISH) (Book #5)
MAYHEM (AND HERRING) (Book #6)

ADELE SHARP MYSTERY SERIES
LEFT TO DIE (Book #1)
LEFT TO RUN (Book #2)
LEFT TO HIDE (Book #3)
LEFT TO KILL (Book #4)
LEFT TO MURDER (Book #5)
LEFT TO ENVY (Book #6)
LEFT TO LAPSE (Book #7)
LEFT TO VANISH (Book #8)
LEFT TO HUNT (Book #9)
LEFT TO FEAR (Book #10)
LEFT TO PREY (Book #11)
LEFT TO LURE (Book #12)
LEFT TO CRAVE (Book #13)
LEFT TO LOATHE (Book #14)
LEFT TO HARM (Book #15)
LEFT TO RUIN (Book #16)

THE AU PAIR SERIES
ALMOST GONE (Book#1)
ALMOST LOST (Book #2)
ALMOST DEAD (Book #3)

ZOE PRIME MYSTERY SERIES
FACE OF DEATH (Book#1)
FACE OF MURDER (Book #2)
FACE OF FEAR (Book #3)
FACE OF MADNESS (Book #4)
FACE OF FURY (Book #5)
FACE OF DARKNESS (Book #6)

A JESSIE HUNT PSYCHOLOGICAL SUSPENSE SERIES

THE PERFECT WIFE (Book #1)
THE PERFECT BLOCK (Book #2)
THE PERFECT HOUSE (Book #3)
THE PERFECT SMILE (Book #4)
THE PERFECT LIE (Book #5)
THE PERFECT LOOK (Book #6)
THE PERFECT AFFAIR (Book #7)
THE PERFECT ALIBI (Book #8)
THE PERFECT NEIGHBOR (Book #9)
THE PERFECT DISGUISE (Book #10)
THE PERFECT SECRET (Book #11)
THE PERFECT FAÇADE (Book #12)
THE PERFECT IMPRESSION (Book #13)
THE PERFECT DECEIT (Book #14)
THE PERFECT MISTRESS (Book #15)
THE PERFECT IMAGE (Book #16)
THE PERFECT VEIL (Book #17)
THE PERFECT INDISCRETION (Book #18)
THE PERFECT RUMOR (Book #19)
THE PERFECT COUPLE (Book #20)
THE PERFECT MURDER (Book #21)
THE PERFECT HUSBAND (Book #22)
THE PERFECT SCANDAL (Book #23)
THE PERFECT MASK (Book #24)
THE PERFECT RUSE (Book #25)
THE PERFECT VENEER (Book #26)

CHLOE FINE PSYCHOLOGICAL SUSPENSE SERIES

NEXT DOOR (Book #1)
A NEIGHBOR'S LIE (Book #2)
CUL DE SAC (Book #3)
SILENT NEIGHBOR (Book #4)
HOMECOMING (Book #5)
TINTED WINDOWS (Book #6)

KATE WISE MYSTERY SERIES

IF SHE KNEW (Book #1)
IF SHE SAW (Book #2)
IF SHE RAN (Book #3)
IF SHE HID (Book #4)
IF SHE FLED (Book #5)

IF SHE FEARED (Book #6)
IF SHE HEARD (Book #7)

THE MAKING OF RILEY PAIGE SERIES
WATCHING (Book #1)
WAITING (Book #2)
LURING (Book #3)
TAKING (Book #4)
STALKING (Book #5)
KILLING (Book #6)

RILEY PAIGE MYSTERY SERIES
ONCE GONE (Book #1)
ONCE TAKEN (Book #2)
ONCE CRAVED (Book #3)
ONCE LURED (Book #4)
ONCE HUNTED (Book #5)
ONCE PINED (Book #6)
ONCE FORSAKEN (Book #7)
ONCE COLD (Book #8)
ONCE STALKED (Book #9)
ONCE LOST (Book #10)
ONCE BURIED (Book #11)
ONCE BOUND (Book #12)
ONCE TRAPPED (Book #13)
ONCE DORMANT (Book #14)
ONCE SHUNNED (Book #15)
ONCE MISSED (Book #16)
ONCE CHOSEN (Book #17)

MACKENZIE WHITE MYSTERY SERIES
BEFORE HE KILLS (Book #1)
BEFORE HE SEES (Book #2)
BEFORE HE COVETS (Book #3)
BEFORE HE TAKES (Book #4)
BEFORE HE NEEDS (Book #5)
BEFORE HE FEELS (Book #6)
BEFORE HE SINS (Book #7)
BEFORE HE HUNTS (Book #8)
BEFORE HE PREYS (Book #9)
BEFORE HE LONGS (Book #10)

BEFORE HE LAPSES (Book #11)
BEFORE HE ENVIES (Book #12)
BEFORE HE STALKS (Book #13)
BEFORE HE HARMS (Book #14)

AVERY BLACK MYSTERY SERIES

CAUSE TO KILL (Book #1)
CAUSE TO RUN (Book #2)
CAUSE TO HIDE (Book #3)
CAUSE TO FEAR (Book #4)
CAUSE TO SAVE (Book #5)
CAUSE TO DREAD (Book #6)

KERI LOCKE MYSTERY SERIES

A TRACE OF DEATH (Book #1)
A TRACE OF MURDER (Book #2)
A TRACE OF VICE (Book #3)
A TRACE OF CRIME (Book #4)
A TRACE OF HOPE (Book #5)

PROLOGUE

Brooke Perkins frowned at the screen in front of her, tapping her fingers on the desk. She'd seen an opportunity, and she was taking it.

"It's time to kill," she murmured. "You are going to be killed, maimed, and destroyed. By the time I'm done with you, there won't be a breath of life left. You will be annihilated."

She nodded in satisfaction, her blond, wavy hair bobbing around her as she reached for the sparkling white keyboard.

She was speaking figuratively, of course, although she hoped the result would be as final as if it was real. But this needed to be done.

Brooke was embroiled in a discussion on social media that had been heading rapidly downhill. It was now firmly in 'argument' territory. The key person speaking against her was a passionate, rather incoherent, forty-something woman who had started out sticking to her guns about her opinion, and who was now getting emotional.

"You're nothing but a bully! And you don't respect my opinion!" the woman complained.

"The point of this discussion is to back up your opinion with hard facts. Got any? Or you fresh out?" Brooke smiled as she typed. This woman might be more than ten years older than her, but Brooke was smarter, and she typed quicker too.

"I have given you facts! I explained to you exactly why our society doesn't respect the elderly. You are ignoring them!"

"Nope, sweetie. No trace of facts in what you said. Your own granny's experience doesn't count, btw. Surely you know that? Give me proof that backs up this deranged theory of yours. Or admit defeat, maybe?"

"You are just trolling now! Why should I give you proof all over again?"

Logic had long ago gone out the window for her opponent on this thread. It was time to end it now.

So far, Brooke had been relatively polite. But now, she was bored of this woman's blathering, and it was time for the gloves to come off.

The early morning sun was gleaming in through a gap in the blinds. Reaching out, she closed the gap, which would otherwise allow for a glare on her screen in a few minutes.

She picked up her coffee cup and sipped.

Mrs. Emotional. She'd seen her before—not the same person, but in numerous guises. All the same type, though. All easily triggered. All illogical in their mindset and beliefs. All easily baited. Brooke couldn't help but be amused. It just so happened that this Mrs. Emotional lived in New Hampshire, a neighbor to herself in Massachusetts, but clearly a world away.

But as fun as this had been, it was time to shut it down now.

Faintly, she heard the buzzer for the apartment below her. She was on the second floor, but her apartment occasionally picked up the noise from below. She frowned as she heard the piercing, distinctive sound intrude on her thoughts.

She'd been able to tune it out most times, but now she couldn't help wondering if these downstairs people were going to get regular visitors so early. Something to keep an eye out for, or rather an ear out for. If this happened too often, outside of business hours, she wasn't going to stand for it.

Still, that was a fight for another day and this was her fight for now. With the concept of what she wanted to say clearly in her mind, she turned back to her screen to annihilate Mrs. Emotional.

But then she frowned once more, hearing the distinctive *thud-thud* of footsteps running up the staircase.

Now what was happening?

This was another thing she disliked about this apartment block. It was noisy when people used those stairs. She'd known getting a unit close to the stairs might result in this noise, but it was irritating when it happened.

And why was someone going up?

Suddenly, Brooke realized that was strange. She was used to hearing people pound and patter down the stairs. But she didn't know if she could ever remember someone running up with what was clearly some urgency.

Was it the kids who lived two floors above her? Had one of them forgotten something and was now sprinting up the stairs to get it?

She had their mother's number. She'd had issues with them before. She was now off the apartment's trick-or-treat list after having lost her sense of humor when that happened last year. Noisy kids and noisy dogs had no place in apartment living. That was her view.

Just as she was wondering whether she should put a message on the apartment's group, Brooke heard a noise that got her sitting bolt upright in her chair, with a cold fright suddenly tightening her stomach.

Her apartment door was rattling. Someone—this person who'd just run up the stairs—was now outside it, and it sounded like they were trying to get a key in. Or jimmy it in some way.

"Who's there?" she called. "You got the wrong place!"

But the rattling continued, and there was something frenzied in the sound.

Her adrenaline surging, Brooke grabbed her phone and jumped up from the workstation, rushing through to the hall.

She gasped in a horrified breath. Sure enough, the door was rattling and shaking, and without a doubt, this intruder was trying to force his way in.

In. To her apartment. A break-in. This could be robbery or worse.

She unlocked her phone, and with hands that were now cold and trembling, dialed 911.

Nothing happened. The call didn't connect, and she felt her breathing accelerate. What was going on? Looking down, she saw that she'd misdialed. In her fear she'd pressed a wrong key.

She redialed with shaking hands, wondering if she should be calling 911 at all, or if she should have run and barricaded herself somewhere—the bathroom, perhaps. She wasn't thinking clearly.

What if he did get in?

She'd always thought she was one of those people who would be decisive in an emergency, who would act in the most sensible way. And look at her! Here she was, frozen to the spot with fear and shock, trying to dial 911 who would take time to arrive. When even now, although he wasn't actually trying to bash the door down, she could hear a noise that sounded a lot like the latch working loose.

Her nerve breaking, Brooke turned and ran. She bolted through the hallway, and as she did, she heard the sound she'd dreaded, the sound of nightmares. The front door bursting open.

Gasping in horror, she whirled around.

There was a man in a ski mask, in dark clothing, his tall bulk framed in the open doorway.

"No!" Brooke cried. "No! Please!"

Her phone dropped from her hand. Her legs felt like water. Her mind was a haze of terror.

And the man was determined. He glanced around the apartment. He fixed his gaze on her. And he ran straight toward her.

"No!" Brooke screamed, but the sound was thin and wavering.

She wanted to say more, to plead with him, to beg for her life, to somehow fight him off. Instead, she turned and ran, hoping to make it to the bathroom and lock herself away.

But in three giant strides, he reached her, and then there was no more time.

CHAPTER ONE

Cami Lark was sitting at the desk in her tiny room in the student digs at MIT. Her final-year study projects were piled on the desk. She'd gotten up to date on her studies today, including some intensive work on the famously difficult Operating Systems and Algorithms courses.

As a full scholarship student, she knew she couldn't afford to do anything less than excel. Top of the class was where she aimed for and almost always achieved.

With this work now complete, she was allowing herself to focus on the mystery that had burned at her mind for the past week.

How had someone in the FBI been able to make her sister's case file basically self-destruct when Cami had sneaked into the system to access it?

How was that even possible? More importantly, why had this sneaky program been planted? All she'd eventually gotten was a corrupted mess of random text that she could make no sense of.

"What do u make of it?" she typed, running her hands automatically over the shaven side of her dyed-black, edgy hairstyle, the way she was in the habit of doing when thinking hard. She fiddled with one of her earrings, twisting the silver ring around.

She was in a dark web conversation with an online friend "Amo-1". Amo-1 lived in another country, and she'd never met her in real life and probably never would. But she was someone Cami trusted. They'd shared a lot of information. They'd shared tips on hacking. They'd shared cocktail recipes, tattoo designs, and the occasional chat about the news.

They both had green-eyed avatars. Cami had never seen her friend's real face. She wondered if she really had green eyes, like Cami did. Despite this anonymity, they'd shared enough personal stuff, both above board and the things that shouldn't be spoken about, for Cami to know that this friend would not betray her if she asked for her take on this. Even so, she'd renamed the corrupted file and only sent fragments that would not link directly back to the FBI. Zero-trust was an imperative, she knew.

But she wanted to get Amo-1's opinion because this friend specialized in file repair and retrieval. That was her profession.

"It's like it's been corrupted, but deliberately," the friend typed back. *"I have seen 1000s of corrupted documents and they don't look like this."*

"How would u do that?" Cami asked.

Amo-1 sent back a shrugging emoji. "*Someone programmed it in. Any other info you can get on it?"* she asked Cami.

"Not at the moment," Cami replied. *"Not without causing trouble I don't want."*

"How did you get this file?" Amo-1 asked.

"I can't say," Cami replied.

"You want me to help and you can't say?" This was followed by a string of annoyed emojis. Amo-1 was pissed by this.

"It's not up to me. I would if I could," Cami explained.

There was a pause.

"Someone got something on you?" Amo-1 asked. Cami knew her friend was too perceptive to avoid getting close to the truth. But at least she wasn't still angry.

"Yes. Someone got something big on me. I shouldn't be looking at this but I am," Cami pleaded.

Cami had never thought she'd be in a position to even know about her sister's case file. Or to be able to search for it in the FBI archives. She wasn't supposed to go looking in the archives, but she hadn't been able to resist it when the opportunity came along.

That had happened after her life had been turned upside down in the shocking turn of events that had seen her co-opted into the FBI to help with a case.

It had all started when she'd hacked their official website to protest about what she saw as their apathy and bureaucracy, based on her personal experience.

After all, the FBI hadn't helped when Jenna had gone missing six years ago. Between them, and her overbearing cop father who'd assumed Jenna was a runaway, the case had never been solved.

But Cami had made one error in her haste to hack the FBI, and it had allowed them to track her.

Never had Cami thought she'd end up being charged with a number of serious crimes and facing a twenty-year jail sentence.

It was the shortage of skills within the organization that had saved her. Three hotshot FBI agents specializing in IT had recently been lured away to work for a startup, leaving the organization with a gap that was hard to fill.

When the FBI had seen her IT ability, the boss in charge at the Boston office, Agent Fraser, had offered her a deal. They would drop the charges if she would help them with a case.

Cami had refused at first, until Fraser had pointed out that she had no right to criticize an organization if she then refused to help when they needed it. So, she'd become part of the team for an intensive couple of days, working for people she'd despised at first, but then, surprisingly, grown to have some respect for.

That short time had changed her life, and her perceptions, in surprising ways. Being co-opted as an IT expert assisting the FBI on an active case had meant she had temporary privileges that had opened her eyes to the reality of crime investigation. As a case partner, having signed sheaves of paperwork, she was authorized to sit in on witness interviews, to actively investigate crimes together with her case partner, to be present at crime scenes, and to handle evidence after it had been correctly processed.

She wasn't authorized to make an arrest or to use a firearm. That was okay, because Cami doubted she could even hit a target with one.

And after this wealth of experience, she had discovered the door was now open to help them again. Skilled agents could not be easily replaced when they left, and with a shortage of tech-savvy manpower, Agent Connor, who'd been Cami's investigation partner, supervisor, and boss on the recent case, had said they might call her in the future.

Cami didn't know what the terms would be if this did happen, or if she would be allowed to refuse. She guessed the alternative this time wouldn't be jail, at least.

"Yeah yeah. Okay I'll stop asking. But still curious," Amo-1 said.

"I'm sorry," she typed, feeling bad suddenly that Amo-1 knew none of this and was trying to help.

"Is it personal to you? This file? Can u at least tell me that?"

"It is personal, and matters to me a lot," Cami said.

"On it," Amo-1 replied.

"Thanks."

There was a pause. Cami reached over and slurped diet soda from the can on the desk. It was room temperature. Pretty yucky. But she was out of coffee, and even though it was nine-thirty a.m., she hadn't yet had a chance to leave her room to buy fresh supplies.

She had a lecture later. Perhaps she'd go on the way back.

"I'm seeing something weird here," Amo-1 typed.

"What are you seeing?" Cami responded, hoping that her friend could provide insight.

"How well did you cover your tracks when you got hold of this?"

Now, Cami's eyes widened. "What?" she said aloud, the word sounding loud and horrified in her small room.

Suddenly, the environment seemed a lot less homely and a lot more threatening. What was Amo-1 implying?

"What do you mean?" she typed back hastily, a cold feeling in her stomach.

"I'm seeing traces of a program within a program," Amo-1 said.

"What????" Cami replied.

"Just fragments. But it looks a lot like a file trace-and-track program that I've seen a couple of times in the past."

"Say this is not so!"

"It's a problem for you?"

"Super mega problem."

"It's almost definitely there. I'm confirming it now."

"This is bad."

"I'm sorry."

Cami's breath was coming fast. A tracking program? So, the file had been set up to self-destruct when it was accessed, but also contained software that would allow the person looking—herself—to be exposed?

Who had set this up? Who was watching her now?

Her instinctive distrust of the FBI had flared all the way back again when she'd seen this file start to corrupt. And now, it had morphed into absolute paranoia. Someone had seen her. And someone had caught hold of her elusive digital footprint and grabbed onto it, and might have been able to follow her all the way out.

Who was this person?

And more seriously, did they know who she was?

If they did, if they knew Cami's backstory with the FBI and how her relationship with them had started out, she could be in a ton of trouble for this. They might even decide to relook at those dropped charges. Perhaps they weren't really dropped, Cami worried. Perhaps they were just shelved, to use as a threat again when needed.

So, that was it. Her freedom might be over. Her life could be turned upside down and inside out again.

She needed to try and research this debacle. She'd have to be very careful what she did. But now, step by step, as invisibly as she could, she would need to retrace her footprints and try to pick up the trail that Amo-1 had detected.

And see if she could figure out who had followed it. The thought that someone had gave her a sick feeling inside.

At that moment, she jerked in surprise as her phone starting ringing. Quickly, feeling a flash of guilt, she picked up the call, and her stomach sank as she saw the caller ID. There could only be two reasons for this, and neither was welcome in Cami's life. Both reasons, in different ways, could mean she was about to be in a truckload of trouble.

It was Special Agent Connor calling her from the FBI.

CHAPTER TWO

Cami was filled with apprehension as she took the call, messaging a quick *"got to go"* to Amo-1. Why was Connor calling? Was this about Jenna's case file, and had he or somebody else worked out that she'd accessed it?

Did they think she'd destroyed the file? Had that been deliberately set up by someone to point the blame her way? It was a chilling thought.

Swiping to pick it up, Cami told herself she had to keep her nerve. She had to stay calm and assume he didn't know. There was no reason to crack under pressure, still less ahead of time. Until he confronted her with the evidence, she was going to keep quiet.

"Hi. Connor?" she said, staring around the cluttered room with the narrow bed, laptop, and posters and notes on the walls, knowing that this was her comfort zone and there was a strong chance she was going to be dragged all the way out of it.

"Cami Lark, I need you to come in now."

"Come in?"

She knew what it meant, but the question was playing for time. She was trying to gauge Connor's tone. Trying to figure out if she was in trouble, and if so, how bad.

She had a class in three hours. But when she'd previously worked for the FBI, they'd contacted the university and whatever they had said, skipping two days of class had never been mentioned.

"To the Boston office. I need you here. As soon as possible."

He disconnected, just as she was taking a breath to ask something else.

Cami made a face. She'd forgotten exactly how brusque Special Agent Connor was. That bossy, overbearing streak in him made all her hackles raise. It put her straight into "rebellion" mode, reminding her of the way her father had been with her.

She couldn't work out if she was in trouble or not. This whole situation was worryingly unreadable.

Cami had an FBI baseball cap and the jacket she'd been issued when she worked for them two weeks ago. She'd stashed them in her wardrobe. Now, she opened the wardrobe, took them out, and put them on, pushing her hair back under the cap.

She grabbed her laptop and shoved it into her carry-bag, adding a quick change of clothing and her toiletry bag, just in case.

And then, after remembering to put her chargers in the bag, she got on the phone and called a cab to take her to the FBI offices in Maple Street, Chelsea, feeling a blend of anticipation and dread seething inside her as she rushed to the door.

***

Fifteen minutes later, the cab dropped her off outside the FBI Boston offices. She walked up to the modern, glass-fronted building, wondering if she should call Connor, or if she should simply head inside and go to his offices.

As it turned out, neither was necessary. Connor was waiting for her, pacing up and down outside the main entrance as if he was mad at her for being late, despite her having rushed as fast as she could. His strong-jawed face, which reminded Cami somewhat of a bulldog's, looked stern. His dark hair, graying at the temples, was freshly cut, short, and neat.

Again, she felt a flicker of resentment at the institutionalism this represented. She understood why the FBI's rules were necessary—in theory, at least. That didn't mean she embraced their ethos on a personal level. In fact, it was the opposite. She hated not being able to operate the way she needed to. It felt as if she had one hand permanently tied behind her back.

And it made her think that, in the long run, the ethos of a hacker and an FBI agent were pretty much incompatible. Should she even be helping here? Was there anything she could really do?

"Come in," Connor said.

He ushered her impatiently inside, which again caused Cami to seethe on a minor level. She'd gotten here at lightning speed. She literally could not have done it any quicker. The cab had arrived in two minutes and driven straight to the FBI offices' main gate. But he was insinuating through his body language that she'd been dawdling around like a rebellious teen, and that he'd been pacing up and down for hours, like a disapproving dad. That was how she was reading him, at any rate. She couldn't help it.

"What's the issue? Why am I here?" Cami said, as she passed through security.

"You're needed in a meeting. With Fraser. We're late, so we need to get moving."

His tone wasn't as harsh as she'd expected, and Cami wondered if she'd read too much into his demeanor. He looked tense, driven, and anxious to get started. *Maybe she was the one who needed to stop taking everything so personally,* she reminded herself. Connor, though not the easiest person to work with, wasn't her dad, and she had to stop thinking about him with the same resentful attitude.

He hustled toward the elevator and she followed, walking as fast as she could, remembering that this brusqueness was just Connor's way. He wasn't one for sympathy, flowery words, or small talk. And since he handled such serious crimes, she guessed that shutting his emotions off was also a coping technique for this seasoned agent, and one she should take note of.

But this might not be a crime she was being called in for, Cami reminded herself. *It might be something worse.* She followed Connor into the elevator and they rode up, walking out and turning in the direction of Fraser's offices.

She could hear voices from inside. As they arrived, two other agents were leaving, their faces stern, holding a sheaf of folders and speaking together quietly.

The trim, fit looking Fraser, his hard face serious, was seated at the small conference table in his office. Cami got the impression that even though it was not yet ten a.m., a full day's work had already been done in this busy room.

"Morning, Connor. Morning, Cami. Sit," he said, gesturing to a chair.

Cami sat.

She was sensing that this wasn't personal trouble. His attitude was cluing her in. The way he was speaking to them was hinting at it. And a moment later, he showed her that she was right. For now, at any rate.

"Cami, we're calling you in because we have another case on board that needs IT expertise on a level that we still don't have available in these offices. It's a murder case. A serial. Two victims so far, and the killer is clearly is targeting victims based on their online interactions."

Shocking as it was to hear murder being discussed as a harsh reality at this table, Cami hesitated. Just like that, they assumed that she would say yes to it? Did she have a choice in the matter? What if she was busy? And with her studies, she was busy. Her final exams were looming ahead. Graduation was imminent.

At the same time, Cami acknowledged the way the last case had made her feel inside. She'd gotten very personally caught up in the last case. She'd ended up feeling as if she'd been fighting for the victims and fighting for justice. She'd been surprised by how passionately she'd felt about it, and how much she'd hated the fact that a killer was out there, terrorizing innocent women.

"Do I have a choice?" she asked.

She had wanted to keep the question neutral, but she could see that Connor had been triggered instantly. He drew in a sharp breath, then he glared at her.

Fraser, however, seemed less perturbed.

He laced his fingers together and stared at Cami thoughtfully. There was something in Fraser's gaze, something in the way he was looking at her, that made her feel guilty. It made her feel as if she was a suspect about to be cross-examined.

"It's complicated. Yes, and no. There are other issues I haven't mentioned yet. Issues that I have only just found out about. So, let me update you on those."

He stared at Cami with narrowed eyes.

She waited, not letting him see how nervous she now felt, listening intently as Fraser started to speak.

"There has been opposition, from higher up, to the decision we made to drop the charges."

She saw Connor's lips press together and he turned to her, looking angry.

"But how can they come back and ask you to relook at something like that? Surely if charges are dropped, they are dropped?" she asked, feeling shocked.

"Yes. Absolutely. Higher management accepts that. However, what they do not accept, and are now complaining about, is the fact that you only contributed to one case, and for a very short span of time."

Connor nodded, causing Cami to feel another flare of resentment. Why had she thought they had been learning to get along? Now, it seemed like she really was being thrown together with her father all over again.

"They said that for such serious charges to be forgiven and forgotten, there needs to be a longer time frame in place. That you should be on call to the FBI for a certain period of time. A year is what they suggested. This memo arrived on my desk this morning. Incidentally, within an hour of the FBI being notified of this new serial case."

A year?

Cami stared at him in horror. One case had felt like a doable time frame, something she could manage. But a whole year? That felt endless. And what if they decided, after a year, that another year was needed? This could end up being like lifelong indenture!

She didn't know what this would mean in terms of her future career. Her lecturers had said there were already a few startups keen to make her a job offer once she'd graduated, but what would a startup think of their new employee calling into work first thing, to say she wouldn't be coming in because she was helping the FBI for an unspecified amount of time, without a choice in the matter? It might jeopardize her career prospects.

"I don't think that's fair. Moving the goalposts like that. What if they keep doing it?"

But Fraser shook his head.

"There's a precedent in the past. A similar situation. That's what they stated as an example. That individual was on call for a year with their particular skill."

"And after the year?"

"They were free to go. No charges, no trouble. We went our separate ways," Fraser said.

"A year might not even mean that many cases, if we can get some decent agents on board. It's still a cop-out, if you ask me," Connor rumbled, clearly in a bad mood with Cami for her brief show of defiance.

"I had to agree with them. A year of being on call when required is reasonable. You have no idea of the political and reputational fallout we suffered from the site being down. For you, it was a few minutes of mischief and payback. For us, it's had major implications."

"It has?" Cami said warily.

"I can tell you now that the meeting time I have had to schedule to thrash this topic out is now running on around thirty hours. Thirty hours in meetings that have been directly caused by what you did to the site. Excluding three flights to Washington DC, Virginia, and San Francisco for top-level security briefings. You can add those hours in, and then we're well over sixty hours. And there are still more to come. Truthfully, it's time I don't have. Time I would rather be spending getting my job done, looking after my team and fighting crime. But that's what has happened, and that's what I've had to handle, because it just so happens that you were a resident of Massachusetts when you committed the crime, so it's my jurisdiction."

"You see?" Connor asked, looking at her angrily.

Cami saw. She hadn't realized the wasted time would be such a factor. It wasn't her actions so much as the repercussions from them.

Fraser had been hit hard by this. By what she'd done. And even though the rebel in Cami wanted to rage against the unfairness of moving the goalposts, she also knew she couldn't act like a spoiled brat over this.

She needed to swallow her pride and take some of the fall for this, just as Fraser had been forced to do.

"I see," she said. "I didn't realize."

"Why should you realize when it's clear you don't respect the organization at all?" Connor grumbled.

Gritting her teeth, Cami ignored him. He was seriously trying to rile her. She couldn't let that happen.

"In that case, I'll agree to the year. I think it's fair."

Fraser's nod of approval coincided exactly with the frown finally leaving Connor's face. Then Cami thought of another possible complication.

"But what if a case comes in while I'm doing my final exams?"

"We'll handle it," Fraser said, in tones that left her with no doubt that he would. "Then there was another issue."

Now, Cami tensed inwardly. Would this be the breadcrumb trail that would clue the FBI to the fact that she'd been looking into their archives?

But Fraser then shook his head. "Actually, I'm not ready to discuss that yet. I want to look into it more closely first."

The knot in Cami's stomach twisted tighter. She was feeling more and more sure that it was this. And since the FBI had now shown their ability to move goalposts as it suited them, she felt extremely worried about what this would mean.

"For now, I need you to get started on this case," Fraser said decisively. "Connor, do you want to review it in your office? I'll have all the documentation sent through." He checked his watch. "I have to go catch a plane."

They stood up, and Cami followed Connor to his office, feeling as if this meeting had ended with a less than stellar outcome.

They'd gotten off on the wrong foot all over again the second time around, and now there was a serial killer case to solve.

Connor's office was a lot like his personality, Cami decided, as she walked inside the small office with a large window, a few doors down from Fraser's. It was businesslike, impersonal, and old-school in its décor and style.

The office was decorated in shades of cream and brown and had a large wooden desk with a dark leather chair, wooden bookshelves, and filing cabinets. The bookshelves were filled with volumes that she knew without even looking were going to be rigorously work-related.

The only touch of color was a vase filled with brightly colored flowers that stood on one of the cabinets.

Cami remembered, when they'd last worked together, that she'd looked up his personal life and seen he was dating an interior designer. Since she was based in Virginia, where Connor had recently worked before being abruptly transferred back to Boston, Cami guessed their relationship was long-distance now.

Were the flowers from her, just because? Or was there a reason for them? A birthday, a relationship milestone?

She wasn't going to ask, because she knew Connor wasn't in the mood to answer. Right now, he was one hundred percent focused on the case ahead. She didn’t think small talk would be well received, and to be truthful, Cami herself wasn’t great at it either. So perhaps, she told herself wryly, she and Connor had more in common than she wanted to acknowledge.

He sat down at his desk, indicating a chair on the other side for Cami to take, and opened his laptop.

"They've emailed through the details," he said gruffly. "Seems the file is still being prepared."

"What are the details?" Cami asked, trying to put her internal thoughts aside and focus on the job.

"Two women have been murdered in the Boston area and surrounds. Both stabbings. Their homes and apartments have been broken into, but the killer has been in and out of the buildings and the area extremely fast. Nobody's seen anything. There's no camera footage so far. It seems he's got a good idea of the layout of the areas where he operates. The escape routes, the neighbors, where cameras are. So, these crimes are quick, dirty, and well-researched."

Now that Connor was in the familiarity of his work mindset, he was sounding more animated and less aggressive.

"Why is tech expertise needed?" Cami asked, hoping this question wouldn't make Connor mad all over again. But he seemed to think it was a reasonable question.

"It's because both of the victims were online at the time of their death. Involved in arguments, discussions, or interactions."

"And how do you know this is deliberate? Why is it related?" Cami pushed.

"Because each time, before he left the premises, the killer wrote in the comments in the conversations they were busy with. He wrote on their own devices, under their name and profile, before he got the hell out of their homes. Just three words, in caps, the same for each victim. 'I'M DEAD. GOODBYE'."

Cami's eyes widened. That was creepy in the extreme.

Without a doubt, the killer had known his victims were online. But how had he known, and what was his reason for targeting these two so far?

Feeling mystified, she took the sheaf of pages that Conner handed her, hoping that she could start to join the dots that would connect, eventually, to the killer.

And then, Connor threw her all over again.

"You can read them in the car," he told her. "We're heading out."

"Where are we going?" she asked, jumping to her feet because he was already marching out from behind the desk.

"To the latest crime scene. It was only reported to us an hour ago, and it's still open. There may be evidence that can help us there. Come on. We can't waste any time." Ignoring her horrified face, he strode past her, heading for the door.

CHAPTER THREE

Nerves churned inside Cami's stomach as she headed to the unmarked car and got in beside Connor. This was exactly where she hadn't wanted to end up. On the way to a crime scene, a stabbing? What would she find there? How bad would it be?

Hoping to distract herself from these unsettling thoughts, she paged through the papers that Connor had handed over, trying to familiarize herself quickly with this case.

"I'M DEAD. GOODBYE." That was chilling. It definitely pointed to a deliberate targeting, and Cami was wondering if it was linked to the victims' online interactions at all. Were they all on the same portal or site at the time? Hopefully this information, still warm from the printer, would supply the details.

"Give me the rundown," Connor commanded as he accelerated out of the parking lot and through the main gate.

"The most recent victim lived alone. We're headed to her apartment building. Her name's Brooke Perkins."

"Is that a common factor? Living alone?" Connor questioned.

Quickly, Cami paged through, looking for answers.

"No. The first victim, Cleo Booth, lived in a house shared with a housemate who wasn't home at the time. And the two victims lived in different areas of Boston. About six miles apart."

"Any other possible links? What did they do for a living?" Connor asked.

"Cleo is a journalist. Or rather, was," Cami corrected herself.

"Interesting," Connor said, and Cami knew he was wondering if her journalism might have led to her being targeted.

"Brooke was a blogger who specialized in social media commentary."

"So, both writers. Anything controversial?"

"It doesn't say here, but I can find out."

Cami got her phone out and went looking.

"Not Brooke. At least, it doesn't say so, but I'll check. I think Cleo might have handled exposes and the like."

Wondering what Brooke had gotten up to, Cami went hunting through her social media portfolio, and she took a look at her likes and involvement online as well.

She seemed to represent a range of clients, and she was active and vocal on a number of wildly various pages. She seemed to have opinions on anything from the Boston food scene to people's attitudes to technology and current events. Some of it, Cami guessed, was controversial. Most seemed to be chit-chat and getting into arguments, the way ninety percent of people acted online. Perhaps she was missing something, and they'd need to look into that more deeply.

"We need to fit together all the pieces. Understand how one of these crimes is related to the other. That's the goal."

"Yes, Connor," Cami said, though she wasn't so sure it would be easy. This killer had clearly done research. Thorough research. He'd known these victims were alone at the time, and he'd been able to get in and out and make his kill without anyone noticing. And in broad daylight too. This last crime had taken place just a couple of hours ago.

So, he was unafraid. He was smart. And currently he was several moves ahead, a situation she now wanted to change as badly as Connor did.

"Here we are," he said.

Cami's head jerked up.

Connor stopped outside a smart, five-story apartment building in one of the older areas of downtown. Already, Cami saw that the murder was drawing the crowds who were gathering, looking curious and shocked. Several police vehicles were parked outside the entrance, and she could see a police officer stationed in the lobby.

As she watched, a white van that she guessed was the coroner's van pulled away.

Cami held her breath, hoping against hope that the van had taken the victim's body away. Perhaps they had picked up everything they needed to from the scene. She hoped so. Viewing a dead body at the scene of the crime ranked right up there with her worst-ever personal scenarios.

Connor climbed out and strode into the lobby, with Cami rushing behind. She was trying to take in the scene. A gracious apartment block with a smart, imposing entrance and pillars outside. A varnished desk in the lobby. A shocked-looking doorman was standing behind it, being questioned by one of the local police.

Where had he been when this happened, Cami wondered. *How had the killer gotten past him?*

From the young man's stunned, traumatized expression, Cami didn't personally think that he could have been part of this, although she was sure that Connor's questioning would rule that out in due course. She was sure that a killer who was clever enough to get in and out of two murder sites without being noticed was also clever enough to take advantage of a gap when the doorman was away from his desk or had gone to the bathroom.

"We'll have a word with him later when the police are finished. Let's go up and take a look at the scene. This was on the second floor," Connor said. "I'm guessing the killer took the stairs."

Were there any cameras? Thinking of how technology could help her, she had a look.

Yes. There was a camera in the lobby. Now that was useful. That was something she could take forward.

"We'll need to request that footage," Connor muttered, heading for the stairs. Another policeman was coming down. He greeted Connor by name, and they exchanged pleasantries. Cami didn't miss how warm Connor sounded. It was literally just her that rubbed him the wrong way. And she was his supervisee and partner. How unfortunate was that?

Her mind went briefly back to the young agent, Ethan, who she'd met on her last case. Ethan was also on Connor's team, though not working directly with him most of the time. Ethan was cute and smart, and he was not a typical FBI agent at all. Cami had liked him a lot.

But Ethan wasn't here. She didn't know where he was. Perhaps he wouldn't be assigned to this case at all. As she tramped upstairs behind Connor, she knew that she needed to resign herself to that likelihood.

There was a hushed atmosphere as they approached the scene itself. Yellow crime scene tape blocked the way to the second apartment from the stairwell. Connor ducked under it, and Cami did the same, feeling her stomach twist again.

There were a few people watching from near the elevators. Other occupants of the apartment, she guessed. Perhaps they had seen or heard something. She wished she could peel off and speak to them, instead of heading into the place where the crime had occurred.

"Let's see how the land lies," Connor muttered to himself, sounding positive and motivated about where they were going.

Cami didn't think she would ever get used to this. She didn't want to. It felt like prying to walk into a dead woman's private space and snoop around, looking for clues in her personal life and possessions.

Although to be fair, Cami acknowledged she did the same online. Online, she was quick to see where she could get a gap and how she could move into people's personal data. *So maybe,* she told herself firmly, *she should get a grip and realize this was exactly the same.*

It just felt more immediate and impactful because she was there, stepping up to the door of the small apartment.

The first thing she saw, to her utter relief, was that the body had been moved. It was no longer where the case report had described it—lying face-down on the far side of the hallway.

"Morning, Connor." A police officer moved quickly forward to greet them as Connor headed for the box where the gloves, head covers, and foot covers were waiting.

Wishing that she wasn't so new and clumsy at doing this, Cami dragged on the items, removing her FBI cap to get the head cover in place. She saw the officer's eyes widen as he took in her hairstyle. Clearly, he was shocked that she was with the FBI with her shaved, dramatic fade, and that moment of amusement briefly eased the stress she felt.

"He forced the door. Fast, brutal," the cop explained. "He must have known what type of lock it was, because he was able to jimmy it open. He came up the stairs; the elevator was on the top floor at the time. Came in, and caught her in the hall. Stabbed her in the back. She was trying to run."

"And the phone?" Connor said. Cami saw where he was looking. The place where the phone had fallen had a number in place. And the phone itself was in an evidence bag, in a box by the door, Cami saw.

"She was trying to dial 911. This we know, because there was a 911 call logged at the time from this location, but the operator reported there was only a scream to be heard."

Cami shivered. That was freaky. She'd tried so hard to call for help. But this had all happened too fast. There hadn't been time.

She had been targeted, efficiently and brutally. Why?

There were two areas that Cami thought she could find answers, fast: the phone and the cameras. The phone was in an evidence bag, and there might be a process to follow to get hold of it.

But the cameras would be quicker. Could she hack in there and take a look?

While Connor was pacing through the apartment, searching for any further clues or evidence in Brooke's living space, Cami decided she would try.

CHAPTER FOUR

There was no way the killer could have accessed this apartment block without passing through the lobby. Cami had seen that when she was downstairs.

And if he had passed through, he would have been under the eye of the cameras. They were angled to cover the lobby effectively. That, too, she'd seen.

Now, how to take a peek at who he was, based on this information?

The security cameras used by this apartment block were a brand called Nuwave. And Cami knew that Nuwave had a design flaw. The user ID was not as secure as it should be. It was accessible if you injected a line of code into the command center. In fact, you could take over the camera that way and actually lock the original user out.

"It's fun to do and impossible to prevent unless you download the camera update," she remembered one of her MIT classmates saying. "And very few people download the update. I mean, who does that?"

Cami didn't want to take control of the camera permanently. But she did want to try and prove her worth to Connor by saving him some time. Bending her head down to her phone, she worked, while vaguely aware of the cops conversing in the next room.

"No sign of any disturbance beyond the lobby?" she heard Connor asking the other cop.

"No. Nothing. He didn't come any further in than the laptop on the desk there, to type the message that's his signature."

"No robbery?"

"Nothing taken that we can see so far. This was a quick kill. In and out, no other reason, seemingly."

"No fingerprints on the keyboard?"

"There were none at the last scene. Only the victim's prints. Same for the door handle. We are going to go through the scene with a fine-tooth comb, but I think this guy is careful and he's worn gloves."

"It seems like the MO doesn't fit with the victim," Connor observed.

"Honestly, to me, the MO looks more like a hit than anything else," the cop said, sounding perplexed and worried. "That's exactly what it seems like. It might not be a professional hit, but for sure, this guy was well prepared."

"What was the cause of death?" Connor asked, and Cami's gaze slid uneasily to that dark stain on the carpet near the far door. That was where she'd died. The body had been moved but the evidence remained. Breathing in, she thought she could smell the tang of blood, a heavy, metallic hint in the air.

"She was stabbed three times in the back. Left side. Long, sharp blade according to the coroner. He was aiming for the heart and clearly got it," the cop said.

"Any sign of the weapon?"

"Nope. He must have brought it with him and taken it away. That would be similar to the last scene. No sign of it there, either. He's not using what's available in the home. There's no time for that."

"What is this guy looking to prove?" Connor muttered, sounding frustrated.

Cami was in. She'd gotten past the basic firewall, and she'd accessed the code. And sure enough, they hadn't updated it. Because nobody ever did. Why would you bother updating a patch on a security camera when it was faithfully doing its basic daily function of recording footage?

Nobody thought that a camera could or would be hacked. Nobody worried about what the implications could be.

Here was the footage. She'd found the archives. Cami scrolled back from the present time, moving through the history. She saw cops first. Cops flooding the footage. Cops were most recently on the scene.

Going back further, she saw a middle-aged woman walking out, holding her purse, presumably on her way to work and with no idea that a serious crime had just played out in her own apartment building.

Another woman left, holding the hand of a young child. As the clock ticked back toward eight a.m., a man in a courier's uniform came in, and for a moment, she wondered if he could be the killer, but then saw him greet the doorman, shaking his hand as if they knew each other.

And then, there he was. Cami caught her breath as she saw him.

Dressed in dark clothing and wearing a baseball cap, bulky jacket, and had a scarf bundled around his face. He kept his head down, walking fast and purposefully. There was nobody at the front desk. He pressed the buzzer for one of the apartments and spoke briefly into the intercom.

Then the security gate clanged open, and he strode up the stairs.

She kept watching, her heart in her throat, but he turned before the building's furthermost camera could get a clear shot of his face. The angle wasn't right. It was as if he knew that he was being watched and having found the blind spot, he'd positioned himself to walk through it.

But she'd seen enough.

Under his scarf and cap, she thought the killer was tall, built like an athlete, with broad shoulders. He walked with purpose, showing no hesitation or fear.

Cami felt short of breath watching this. There was something about his ferocious intent that chilled her blood. This creep was an obsessed killer. He had to be.

But why had that gate opened up for him, allowing him to stride so confidently through it?

He surely couldn't have rung Brooke's bell?

Nope, the timing would not have allowed for that. If he'd rung her bell with a plausible excuse, she would have opened the door for him. He wouldn't have had to force his way in, and she wouldn't have had time or opportunity to dial 911. She would have come face to face with him, and he could have killed her instantly.

But he hadn't done that, probably because she would have asked who he was and refused him entry. So, he must have chosen someone else. Who would that have been, and how did he know that this person would open up? Because it seemed like he had known.

She rewound the video and zoomed in again.

If she looked carefully, could she see his hand move? He'd kept his face away from the camera but not his hand.

In slow motion, Cami looked again as Connor and the other cop returned from the other room.

"Nothing to be found," Connor was saying, sounding frustrated. "Now we have to figure out how he got in. How he got past the lobby."

"Seems that he chose the time when the doorman was called away to open the garage door downstairs. So he must have been watching the building," the cop said. "But still, to get past that security door, someone must have opened up for him and buzzed him in."

"He wouldn't have rung her bell. If he had, she wouldn't have had time to dial 911," Connor said, echoing Cami's thoughts.

"That's going to be a big job, since there are thirty-five apartments in this complex," the cop said.

"We'll start with the ones at the front and try to work our way through. Still, by the time we've done that, we might be trying to figure out where this guy is now rather than where he came from."

Cami hit "Pause" and turned to look at him. "What if I could find that out for you? Would it save you time?"

"It would depend how much time it would take you," Connor said, sounding grumpy and unappreciative of her efforts. "We have a lot to do. We can't waste hours trying to get this information. Sometimes, feet on the ground is quicker."

"I've got it here," she said, feeling a momentary satisfied pleasure at the shock on his face. "To me, it looks like he rang the bell for number three. Take a look and tell me what you think."

CHAPTER FIVE

Five minutes later, Cami was standing half a step behind Connor as he knocked on the door of apartment number three. She felt pleased to have figured this out. Not only did they now have—at least—an idea of the killer's height and build, but they also knew how he'd gotten in, and that might just take them further.

At any rate, she felt hopeful as she heard footsteps approach.

"Who's there?" a woman's nervous voice asked.

"FBI," Connor called out. He held his badge up to the peephole in the door.

A stressed-looking woman in her mid-thirties opened the door, holding her young son's hand. Her face looked pale and make-up free, and her hair was tied back in a rough ponytail. But she was wearing a beautifully embroidered top, her nails were neatly done, and the apartment behind her looked well decorated, with wall tapestries, beadwork ornaments, and colorful hand-knotted rugs.

Her gaze rested upon Connor and then slid curiously to Cami. She looked fearful. Her expression was wary.

"FBI Special Agent Connor," Connor introduced himself briefly. "Ma'am, we need to talk to you." He glanced at her son.

"Go to your room," she said, turning the boy around and giving him a pat on the back.

Connor waited until he was out of sight before continuing.

"I don't know if you're aware there has been a murder upstairs?"

The woman put a hand to her neck as if that knowledge hurt her.

"I heard earlier," she said in a shaking voice. "The doorman said someone had been killed. He got hold of me and said I should probably keep the children away from downstairs for a while. But I didn't realize it was someone who lived here! Who was it?"

"Brooke Perkins," Connor said.

Hissing in a shocked breath, she clapped a hand over her mouth.

"No!" she said.

But Cami was surprised that she didn't look as genuinely sad as she'd expected. Shocked, yes. But she didn't look gutted with grief, the way that she'd assumed she might on hearing of a neighbor's death.

Thinking back to the comments she'd read online, Cami was starting to wonder if Brooke had been a difficult person. Someone who wasn't well liked. And perhaps, therein, might lie a clue to her death, she thought.

Connor was plowing forward to the main reason for their arrival on her doorstep. Cami didn't know if he'd picked up what she had.

"Your name, ma'am?" he asked.

"I'm Marlene Somers."

"Did you know the victim well?"

"No. I hardly knew her at all. We must have spoken a couple of times at most, I think."

"And how long have you been here?"

"Two years. She was already here when I moved in."

Cami guessed he was asking these easy questions to steady Marlene up. Because, without a doubt, she had a shock waiting when he told her how the killer had gotten in.

She saw him take a breath and knew it was time. This question was coming. And she knew it would be utterly devastating to this woman, who would probably feel that the crime had been her fault.

"Ms. Somers, this morning, did you let anyone into the building?"

"I—well, yes. I make crafts and homemade items. Jewelry, clothing, home décor. And there are always couriers and delivery people coming in and out to collect." She frowned. "But this morning, I do recall, the buzzer rang, and a courier didn't arrive. He came in about ten minutes later."

"So you let someone in, but they never arrived at your door?"

It was clear that Marlene was putting two and two together. She stared in horror at Connor.

"Was that him? Did I let the killer in?"

Connor shrugged. "We're still working on the timeline. But if you had someone ring your bell who never arrived at your front door, it's likely."

Marlene was now blinking tears away. She looked sheet white. "If I did that, I'll never forgive myself. That's just the biggest catastrophe I've ever heard of. I caused her to be killed?"

Connor shook his head. "Ma'am, without a doubt, Brooke was deliberately targeted. Why, we don't know. This was a carefully researched crime, and if ringing your buzzer hadn't worked, he would have found another way."

"I still—I can't . . ." Tears were now streaming from her eyes.

"Did the man speak to you when you answered the door?" Cami asked.

"Yes. I mean, I wouldn't have let a random stranger in! I said, 'Who's that?' and he said, 'Courier'. That was all. I don't remember him saying anything else. He sounded normal."

"Local? Any accent?"

"Local, I think. I didn't pick up any strange or unusual accent. I wish I'd put two and two together when he didn't arrive, but my phone rang, and my child was crying, and it was just one of those mornings. It went right out of my mind."

Cami glanced at Connor. He looked as if he was thinking hard.

"Is there anything else you can tell us about this man? Anything at all?" Connor asked. "Did you notice a vehicle outside?"

At street level, she might have done, Cami thought. But Marlene shook her head. "I had my curtains closed," she explained.

"Is there any signage outside referring to your business?"

She shook her head. "I'm online, so I don't have signage. The apartment block wouldn't allow it, and in any case, I'm not a shop. I can't have people arriving to look through my stock." *Now that she was talking about her work, she seemed to have settled down,* Cami thought. *She seemed less stressed.*

"So, the only people who know about your business are the couriers and delivery firms?"

"That's correct."

"And how often do you get pick-ups?"

"Almost every weekday morning. I usually get my pickups between seven and nine a.m. One or two different pickups, depending on where stock is going out."

Cami guessed that if someone had observed and researched the building they would have been able to find this out. Perhaps the killer was looking for a way in, and this had just been the easiest. Connor was right, she realized. If this hadn't been available, he would have found another way. His aim was to gain access quickly, kill, and leave.

"Thank you, ma'am. What you've told us has been helpful," Connor said.

"I'm still so shocked. I feel responsible for this. And unsafe too. At the moment I feel as if I should move. Is my family at risk?" she asked in appeal.

Connor gave a quick nod. "We don't know enough yet, so precautions are wise. Please, take care and be on the alert. This is a serial case, and we are still gathering information, but he's struck in two very different areas so far."

Her eyes widened as she heard this news.

"Everyone needs to be careful until this is solved," Connor concluded. "Be aware of who you let in. And make sure you have good front door security. Keep the chain on."

"Will do," she said shakily.

They turned away.

"This guy must have been planning and observing," Cami said as she and Connor walked back to the lobby. "Maybe he even had a way of researching the building online? Given that he tracked the victims online?"

"That's a possibility," Connor agreed, but he didn't sound enthused by her idea.

"You don't think it's likely?"

"There's another possibility, and it's always the first place we start," he told her.

"What's that?"

"It's that this killer was known to the victims. Either one, or both of them, knew him. You'd be surprised how often murders are committed by someone close to the victim. The other one could be a smokescreen, or else the same person could have a link with both. We need to look into the victims' connections before we go any further."

CHAPTER SIX

Immediately after he had spoken the words about the victims' connections, Connor's thoughts went to that phone, nestled in the evidence bag. There would be a wealth of information on Brooke's phone. She might have interacted with the killer on her phone. Especially if she was very active on social media. If the other victim was, too, perhaps that was a common thread.

"Can we look on her phone?" Cami asked.

"Yes, we can." Normally, the phone would be sent to the techs. But he'd already seen enough of Cami's IT ability to know that they might be able to work faster this time, even though the phone would then need to be correctly processed as part of the evidence chain. "Are you able to open it?" he asked.

He made sure to ask question in a matter-of-fact way. As if he didn't doubt Cami's ability to get that phone unlocked and access the information on it, faster than the techs could. Even though he had no idea if she could. It might have been a lucky break the last time. She might not be able to easily repeat that success again.

"Yes. I saw what model it was. It's about a seventy percent chance I will be able to get into at least some of the content fast," she confirmed.

He felt a flare of admiration for the unusual youngster he'd been partnered with. It was strange how he was beginning to understand how her mind worked, even though he didn't allow much of his feelings to show during working hours. Connor had learned it was better to keep the two coldly separate. Experience had taught him that this was a tough, dangerous job, and although loyalty was vital in the FBI, there were perils inherent in getting too close to any partner or colleague. He'd learned that the hard way. The grief in losing a partner who was also a good friend was extreme. Now, Connor preferred to stay behind his walls.

Quickly, he looked back over the basic case notes in the folder to see if they had identified any contacts so far.

"Brooke worked for herself," he told Cami. "The social media business is in her name. And it looks as if her parents are both deceased."

"Does she have any friends or relatives close by?" Cami asked.

Connor shook his head. "Not according to this. She has a sister living overseas, according to the basic records we've accessed. We don't have more than that. She was interacting on a public news site when she was murdered, commenting on an article about elderly people in care homes that was causing some debate."

"So anyone could have seen her there?"

"Yes. Anyone, but the question is, who knew her habits? Did someone know she was likely to be online at that time? Perhaps someone even confirmed she was online. So, we need information on friends, business associates, and if she has a boyfriend. Also, recent messages and calls. While you try to access the phone, I'm going to question the neighbors and see what they can tell us. You do the tech work. I'll do feet on the ground."

He strode away, feeling a mixture of irritation and relief at being paired up with this young tech whiz kid again. She most definitely got under his skin. That was for sure. He battled to align with her "no rules matter" mindset. Having her under his supervision was stressful, because he had no clue what she might do at any given moment. She could do nothing or go completely rogue. She'd committed a crime in the past and didn't seem to adequately care about the difference between legal and illegal. Which was a big worry for him. Because Cami and control just didn't go together. The wrong actions could sink the case or even his career.

But on the other hand, she'd just gotten a look at the camera that had allowed them to see how the perp had gained access. That had saved them some serious time, and she had done it like it was no big deal at all. She wasn't boasting about her skills. It almost seemed that she didn't even think about how special her abilities were.

He was so used to people claiming that they were good at stuff but failing to deliver when put to the test. But not Cami. With her, it was the other way round.

Well, he'd see what progress she made. And now, it was time to see who else was at home, and who in this apartment block knew Brooke.

Connor set off, striding to the door on the right hand side of hers. As he approached it, he had a feeling there was nobody home. The curtains on the small window overlooking the corridor were closed. The place felt quiet.

He knocked anyway.

Sure enough, no response.

He decided to go one apartment further before backtracking and trying the opposite side. Walking on, he saw this was a good decision. Someone was, in fact, home here.

Connor rapped on the door.

A young, dark-haired man came to the door. He looked like someone's student son, Connor thought instantly. He was too young to be renting a place like this himself. This guy looked like he had a day off from class.

And he looked very at ease. The news hadn't traveled this far. However, his eyes widened in surprise to see Connor standing on his doorstep.

"Uh—can I help you? Are you police?" he said with a note of incredulity in his voice.

"FBI," Connor said. "There's been a murder."

Suddenly, the young man's eyes showed fear.

"A murder? You mean—here? In our apartment building?" he exclaimed.

"Correct," Connor confirmed.

"Which one? Who?" The note of panic in his voice was now more intense. "My mom's gonna freak," he muttered.

"Two doors down. Brooke Perkins."

"Her?" He sounded surprised.

"What's your name?" Connor asked.

"Trent Holliday," he said.

"Did you hear anything, Mr. Holliday?" Connor asked. "It happened earlier in the morning. Probably three and a half hours ago."

The man shook his head. "I was doing an online tutorial, I had headphones in. When it finished, I went straight onto the work assignment and played music. So, I haven't been aware of much of anything this morning."

"You might need to listen out, if you're home alone, until this case is solved," Connor warned.

"Yes. Yes, I see that. It's scary. Two doors down?"

He watched as the man shuddered, thinking clearly of what might have happened inside her apartment and what must have gone down during the murders.

"Did you know her?" Connor asked.

Now, Trent looked cautious. Hesitant, almost. "Not really," he said.

"You don't seem too sure about that," Connor replied.

Trent looked down. Fidgeted. "I don't think I should say this," he muttered.

"Say what, son. Remember, if it might help save another life, I need to hear it." Connor planted his feet in the doorway and waited.

"Well, she was . . . she wasn't an easy person. She was difficult. She had issues with everything. I came home late a couple of weeks ago, and she heard me walking past. The next day, she'd emailed a complaint to my mother. I know a lot of people were scared of her. She could get really hardcore. So yeah, I mean, I don't know who will tell you this. Maybe it has to be me, and I didn't even know her well, but she wasn't the most popular person in this building. That's for sure."

"I appreciate what you've told me."

Connor felt troubled as he took this in.

Usually, everyone in this young man's situation would be eager to speak well of the deceased, unless they had a serious gripe against them that was public knowledge. And even then in that situation, it was usually soft-soaped.

But to come out with such a statement, as a random acquaintance, meant that the victim really had not gone out of her way to make friends. And in fact, that she might have gone out of her way to cause trouble. Some people were like that. And as an investigator, it made the job a lot harder when those people were killed.

"Was there anyone in these apartments she was close to?" he asked.

But Trent shook his head. "I don't know of anyone. But then, I didn't know her well. I heard people talking, though, when she'd filed a complaint. And she did that often. There's a social media group, and she was on it occasionally, again, to complain. She didn't seem friendly with anyone, or bad enemies with anyone."

"Did you see her get any visitors?"

Again, the headshake. "I didn't notice. Honestly, I just stayed out of her way. It was easiest. You get these people in every apartment community, I think. There's no sense in fighting."

Connor thanked him and turned away, feeling troubled. It didn't seem like Brooke had tried to be likeable or neighborly at all. And the fact that she'd acted this way to people in the same building meant a longer list of suspects. People were consistent, that was one of his personal truths in life. And it seemed as if Brooke had treated her neighbors and fellow residents consistently badly.

He knocked on the two doors on the opposite side, but it seemed that at this hour, most of the neighbors were out or at work. This was a working neighborhood.

And he somehow doubted that Brooke had many close friends here. It seemed she'd kept to herself and wanted others to do likewise. Therefore, the only quick route to finding her connections was going to lie with the phone, and suddenly he hoped very hard that Cami had managed to get into it.

He hurried back downstairs to the lobby, where she was sitting in a corner behind the counter and working on it. Connor made a quick detour and spoke to the doorman, but the conversation only confirmed that he remembered Brooke having few visitors here in recent weeks, although she went out a lot and received the occasional delivery.

Then, Connor heard Cami give a gasp of triumph. He rushed over, and she looked up at him, her face alight, and her eyes animated.

"I didn't think I was going to get in. I only just managed," she said. "And there seems to be a lot of texts here. I can’t find anything bad or threatening so far, but I can look more closely. I’ve been mainly looking for connections.”

“Have you found any?”

“There’s a lot of work interactions that are impersonal and quite short. She dealt with a lot of clients.” Connor watched as Cami scrolled back.

“Here’s something.” She sounded relieved. “Recent messages with a friend that she chatted to regularly, according to the chain I’m seeing here."

"Who's that friend?" Connor asked, feeling a surge of hope that they had at last found someone Brooke was on a cordial footing with.

"Her name's Barbie. And according to the texts, she lives in Boston," Cami said. "I'm guessing that means they hung out together." She glanced down at the phone again. "Yes. They met up just a few days ago, I can see their arrangements were made here."

"Find out where she lives," Connor said, feeling reluctantly pleased that Cami had been able to get them on the next important step.

He wanted to get face to face with Barbie, and the sooner, the better.

CHAPTER SEVEN

Barbie Pratt lived in Seaport District, one of the more expensive areas in Boston. Cami couldn't find any work details for her, only for her husband, Ed Pratt, who worked for an architectural firm.

"I imagine Barbie's a housewife or a homemaker?" Connor asked as they climbed into the car. "I guess we go straight to her home and hope we find her there."

"She might work part time, or for a charity, or run a business from home," Cami suggested, feeling annoyed by his assumption.

"Yeah, a possibility," Connor agreed, pulling out on to the road, but there was a tone in his voice that hinted otherwise.

"You think you're right and I'm wrong?" she challenged him.

"Let's just say I've been on cases in this area before, and this is how I see it. I'm playing the percentages here," Connor said flatly, causing Cami's hackles to rise again.

Even if he was right, why did he have to be so "my way or the highway" about it, she seethed.

But she had to acknowledge Connor's experience here and that he had a profile of what to expect in this area. Cami had never spent time there and had only driven through it on a couple of occasions. She'd grown up in Mattapan. That was where her dad had worked, in one of the city's rougher neighborhoods. It was where she guessed he still lived, with her mother, in the small house with the tiny yard at the end of the street, bordering the derelict factory.

She hadn't been back home for a long time. Cami had resolved, after Jenna had disappeared, that she was going to make her own way in life and not ask her parents for a thing. She didn't want to feel in debt to them. Not when her father had a way of dangling such obligations over her head like a blade.

She would rather break ties with them, sad as it made her. But she knew Jenna's disappearance had affected them all in different ways, and once again, Cami felt a sense of dread as she thought about that folder, and the way it had erased itself.

Why? Who was behind it, and what details had they not wanted her to see?

Worse still, did they now know who she was?

Pushing away those unsettling thoughts, she turned her attention back to the road, because they were now turning into Broadside Street, where Barbie lived.

"This is her place." Connor stopped outside an elegant, stone-clad home set in a lushly treed yard, with a profusion of flower beds. "Now, let's go see if she's home." He climbed out of the car and turned back to Cami. "Remember, she might not yet know her friend's dead."

Cami decided that breaking the news about death must be one of the worst parts of being with the FBI. She walked along the neat stone path behind Connor, feeling uneasy about what to expect as he rang the doorbell.

Cami was wondering if a housemaid or an au pair or even a butler might answer the door in this fancy neighborhood, but it was opened by a woman who matched the ID photo she'd seen. Barbie was petite, with streaky blond hair and piercing blue eyes.

She was dressed in yoga pants. *Points to Connor,* Cami thought reluctantly.

"Can I help you?" she asked.

"Mrs. Pratt?" Connor asked, his voice solemn.

"That's me," she said, a tiny frown spoiling the perfection of her forehead.

"I'm FBI Agent Connor. There's been a murder," he said as he showed his badge, getting to the point in a harsh but efficient way. "Sorry to tell you this, but Brooke Perkins was killed this morning. That's why we're here. We're investigating her death, and I understand you knew her well."

Barbie actually took a physical step back, staggering onto the richly colored rug in the hall, leaning forward with her shoulders bowed.

"No! No!" She stared at Connor again, eyes wide, seeming almost to be pleading with him. "This can't be right. She's my good friend."

Connor gave her a minute, while Cami looked around the house, feeling uncomfortable to watch Barbie as she leaned against the wall, her head in her hands, and sobbed.

She could see a living room through the archway, decorated in steel blue and slate gray. The house was very modern, very minimalist. It seemed like a calming environment.

"What happened?" Barbie asked in a wobbly voice, finally getting her shock under control.

"There was a break-in at her home this morning. She was stabbed. It doesn't look like a robbery. It follows on from a similar crime nearby, a few days ago."

"A serial killer?" Now Barbie's face was pale. “I remember hearing something about that today, but I didn’t listen, and I don’t think there were details given. They definitely didn’t mention Brooke. Why her?”

"We don’t yet know," Connor said. "We’re getting as much information as we can, and we're looking for background on her life and contacts."

Barbie suddenly seemed to pull herself together as if this request had been a call to action.

"Please. Come in," she said.

A minute later, they were sitting in the living room, which showcased paintings and memorabilia that Cami thought must be from a few different countries. The Pratts were well traveled, she guessed. She recognized what looked like a Moroccan vase, a wooden sculpture that might be Indonesian, and the tapestry on the wall was probably from Japan.

"This is such a shock. I literally can't believe it. We had drinks together only a few days ago," she said, her voice shaking.

"How long have you known her?"

"For years. We were good friends at school. Then we fell out of touch. We went to different colleges. I got married. And then just a couple of years ago, we reconnected. If I remember correctly, we actually bumped into each other online and then met up in real life again and saw each other regularly from there." Her face warmed briefly at the memory, before she looked sad again.

"Did she mention that anything was wrong in the past week or two? Share anything that was troubling her?" Connor asked. "Did you have that close a friendship? Would she share personal issues or problems with you?"

Barbie thought for a long moment, as if she was trying to conjure up memories of her last meeting with Brooke. "We did have a good friendship, yes. And we shared a lot. But trouble?" She frowned. "She never mentioned anything was wrong, and I do think if there had been, she would have at least said something. Her work was going well. She was busy. Too busy, she sometimes said."

"Any new relationships?" Connor asked.

"No. She was that busy. She said it was good, that it was keeping her out of trouble," Barbie admitted.

"She spent a lot of time on social media," Cami volunteered, seeing Connor's quick sideways glance as she spoke.

"Yes, well, it was her job," Barbie said, now sounding ever so slightly defensive, as if this might be a criticism, or be leading up to it.

"Did she mention anyone was stalking her online? Harassing her?" Cami asked.

"No. Look, when you're on social media nonstop, you're going to have your share of issues. Not everyone agrees with everyone else, and the best way to start a fight is to state an opinion. But nothing unusual, I would say. She knew how to stand up for herself, that I can say."

Now Connor continued this line of questioning, and Cami thought he was taking advantage of the fact that in her shock, Barbie was almost babbling.

"It seems that she wasn't the easiest person to get on with. Someone in her apartment confirmed that she could be quick to complain and criticize. Do you know if that caused any personal conflicts?"

Barbie stared out of the window for a moment, looking thoughtful.

"No. She was picky, I agree. Quite a perfectionist. And she had strong opinions, sure. But she had such a kind heart. I mean, if you knew her at all, you'd know what a good person she was."

Was she trying too hard with that last statement, Cami wondered as Connor continued.

"Is there anything else you think we should look into? It might even be something further back in her life. Perhaps from a few months ago or even a year ago," he pressed. "Sometimes, issues from the past can raise their heads again and cause problems."

And then, Cami felt a flare of excitement as she saw Barbie nod.

"It was a while ago, but yes. Now that you mention it, I'm remembering she did say something about an ex a couple of weeks ago. That he was reaching out to her again, and she had shut him down. She didn't seem stressed about it, though, more dismissive of him. Like she wasn't going to allow him back no matter how hard he tried."

"Who is he?"

"His name is Roland Coyne. They dated on and off a few years ago, and he made her life miserable for sure. He was emotionally abusive, and although she never said, I suspect that there were physical issues also. She'd just broken up with him for good when we reconnected."

"What happened after the break up?"

"He moved out of Boston, and I think he went south, to Dallas or Houston. He got a transfer from his work. I remember he bragged to her that it was a more senior position, and she'd be losing out. Toxic, you see?"

"What work did he do?" Connor asked.

"He was an accounts manager for a finance firm. Worked for one of the big firms, quite high powered. But a nasty man. In my opinion, he was a narcissist, or even a sociopath." She frowned thoughtfully. "However, he did move away, so I'm not sure that will be helpful."

"It might be. And thank you very much for the information. Connor stood up. "I'm sorry again to have brought you bad news. You take care, and please stay in touch if you think of anything else that might help us." He handed over his business card.

"I will." Barbie's face darkened. "I hope you catch this guy. It's the most terrible thing I ever heard of. Just please, for Brooke, do it."

As soon as they were out of the well-decorated house, Cami was on her phone, researching so furiously that she nearly veered off the stone path and onto the verdant lawn.

"Roland Coyne isn't history," she said, when they reached Connor's car. “And he isn't living in Houston, either.”

"He isn't?" His gaze sharpened as he looked at her.

"What I'm seeing here, from a glance at his social media, is that he's been back in Boston for a couple of months. Since April, in fact. That might be when he started wanting to get in touch with Brooke again." Suspicion surged inside her. Her fingers flew over the keyboard. Getting into the car, she opened her laptop as well and quickly logged in, adding the power of a second device to her search.

"You got an address?" Connor was staring at her expectantly.

"I do," Cami said. “I've found a chunk of information on him, actually. Hang on.”

She could feel Connor seething with impatience as she worked, trying to get more information from the small toehold she'd obtained.

“There was a security glitch a while ago when he used his credit card. It's allowing me to take a peek at some of the transactions. I've got a program that can open this up. Maybe it'll tell us more.”

While on the twenty-minute drive to where he lived, Cami felt determined to find out as much as she could about this suspect. Especially since one unwise purchase on a less-than-secure site had allowed her a window into the other transactions he'd made.

"It started off on a site where he was buying cheap cigarettes," she told Connor, engrossed in her research, barely noticing the twisting and turning of the car as it wound its way through suburbia. "Since then, he's been buying new things for his apartment, and also quite a few items that are raising red flags for me."

"Such as?" Connor asked.

"A delivery of flowers. I'm looking into that. Because it seems they were sent to Brooke's address."

"That so?" Connor sounded interested.

"But I see here it was noted down as 'delivery rejected'. She wouldn't sign for them. She clearly didn't want those flowers, or anything to do with him."

“We’ve got a link to Brooke. That’s a good start, and it provides a reason why a narcissistic man might have gotten angry. Now, what else can you find? Is there any link to the other victim, Cleo?” Connor asked.

Cami looked deeper into the records. Was there anything to be found? Any connection at all between them that could provide a reason for why Cleo had been killed?

"There must be something," she murmured, determined to find out if there was. Her brain raced as she considered various scenarios and researched any links to Cleo’s address.

Then, widening her search, she tried using Cleo’s name.

And finally, something came up. Cami’s eyes widened as she read it. This was a link in a direction she’d never expected.

She’d struck gold, only on a reread, she decided this wasn’t gold.

It was more like dynamite.

CHAPTER EIGHT

"I can't believe this," Cami said. She could hear the incredulity in her own voice.

"You found something?" Connor's voice was sharp, excited.

"I did. Cleo was involved in writing an expose piece listing irregularities at the finance firm that Roland used to work for in Houston."

"Seriously? How long ago?"

"A couple of months back. The firm took a knock for it, for sure. It was an accurate article, I guess. There were a number of resignations, Roland included. He came back to Boston, and got a job with a different firm. A smaller firm. So that's why he moved here again."

"That's a strong link to both suspects in very different ways," Connor agreed. "One victim rejected him, and one wrote a damaging piece."

"Co-wrote," Cami corrected him, wanting to make sure she provided accurate background. "She wasn't the only writer. It looks like about five different journalists were involved in the piece. And Roland was just an employee, even though a senior one. I mean, he wasn't a shareholder, but it must have been a knock for him, moving back. Especially if he has an ego."

He clearly did, Cami thought. His behavior toward Brooke had made that obvious.

"Could be a motive for murder," Connor agreed, and she felt a flare of pride. Quickly, she finished scanning through all his transactions for the last months.

"He's still a big spender. And he spends a lot of money on alcohol. This guy seems to party large," she said. Looking at his purchases, she thought it was painting a picture of a reckless, impulse-driven man who had narcissistic tendencies. She guessed he was a personality type who could kill. What she didn't know was whether he would have had the self-control to plan meticulously. But since he was clearly intelligent, she thought he would have.

A minute later, Connor pulled up outside the offices of Mercer and Marks, the finance firm that Roland now worked for. Even though this was a smaller firm, Cami noted the building's ostentatious, white-painted, pillared frontage, with vines twining up each side of the imposing entrance door.

Walking in, she saw there was clearly no expense spared on the décor. This was all top-end interior design, with sleek, steel-gray leather furniture and a massive plate glass window that overlooked the leafy suburbs beyond.

Connor strode up to the space-age reception console where the receptionist with swept back platinum hair and heavy, dark eye make-up greeted them with a polite, "Good afternoon."

"FBI. We're looking for Roland Coyne," he said.

The receptionist shook her well-coiffed head apologetically.

"I'm afraid Mr. Coyne is not here now. He's at a client function."

Connor pressed his lips together. "And where would that be?"

"At the Connoisseur's Club. But it's a private function," she added hastily, as if regretting she'd spoken in such haste.

"Thank you," Connor said, turning away.

As they strode back to the car, Cami was already looking up the club.

The Connoisseur's Club, it seemed, was a "private function venue" for "upmarket events" located at 182 Cross Street.

"It looks like a conference setup," Cami said. "That's the impression I get. I don't know how big this function is. It sounds as if it might be quite large. The club looks enormous."

She wondered what function Roland was currently attending at four p.m.

"Maybe he's at a training session, maybe an awards function, or maybe a client meet and greet?" Cami guessed.

"Something like that. At least we know where he is," Connor said.

Cami couldn't wait to find out more. This man had links to both victims. He'd been back in town for a couple of months thanks to Cleo's article and had been rejected by Brooke when trying to reconnect with her.

He could have snapped, Cami theorized. This cascade of events, from the work relocation to the rejection, might have triggered a psychotic break that had made him start killing the people he blamed.

She stared again at the photo she'd found of him online, taking him in. He was in his late twenties and surprisingly good looking, with thick, dark hair, strong features, and piercing eyes.

She wondered if his looks had contributed to an ego that wouldn't allow him to suffer rejection or setbacks.

It was time to find out, because here they were, at the Connoisseur's Club.

It was a discreet venue, Cami saw as she got out of the car. Only minimal signage clued the visitor to its presence. Nothing more than a brass sign above a solid looking wooden door, which was set on the corner of a street block containing offices and warehouses.

"Well, this is it," Connor said. "I'm going to go in and find him."

Feeling like a tag along all over again because Connor hadn't said "we," Cami trailed along behind him.

The door was open, but as Connor walked down the short, narrow staircase that led to it, Cami saw that a thickset doorman was standing outside.

"Can I help you?" he asked. He didn't sound welcoming.

"FBI Agent Connor. We need to speak to someone inside. Name of Roland Coyne. He's here?" Connor asked, showing his badge.

The doorman planted his feet firmly and folded his arms.

"Sir, this is private property. And there's a private function going on inside."

"We're here on a murder investigation. It's urgent," Connor countered.

"Guest list only, I'm afraid," the doorman said. "Without a warrant, I'm not authorized. Please stand aside."

He waved Connor over as a few other people arrived, and they moved to the side of the stairs as the newcomers pushed past. Two well-dressed women got ushered through without referring to the guest list at all, Cami noted. A tattooed man dressed in a black sweater, who said he was lights and music, was also allowed in. And then, a man on his own in a business suit had his name checked on the guest list before being waved through.

Then the doorman folded his arms and stood solidly in front of the door again. Cami could see that this was a big problem. The doorman clearly knew his rights and was not going to budge on this. Perhaps he'd had police arrive on his doorstep before, she wondered.

Glancing at the table behind the doorman, she saw that the private function involved live music. A band called The Glamour Girls was playing. That sounded more like a party than a work event, she decided. But they clearly weren't getting in to find out.

Unless she could hack the guest list somehow? Could she do that?

Nope. The doorman was working from a printed page, old-fashioned, clunky, and impossible to hack.

Now what were they going to do? Wait until he came out? From the sounds of things, that might be a few more hours.

"Okay. Thanks."

Connor turned away, ushering Cami ahead of him. They walked around the corner and back to the car.

"Should we look for another way in?" Cami asked. She felt frustrated beyond measure that they were being blocked from entering. If they could find an alternative entrance, that might bypass the problem. Once they were in and questioning Roland, it would be easy enough to leave if they were asked—with him in tow.

"Yes. That's exactly what we need to do now. We must walk around and have a look," Connor agreed.

Keeping out of sight of the doorman, they paced around the building. There was a steel fire door on the side wall, Cami saw, but it was locked from the inside. And there was a staff entrance but that, too, was guarded by a locked security gate.

"Place like this probably does a big turnover in cash sales on the drink," Connor explained. "That's why they're tight on security. They don't want robberies or staff running away with the takings."

"So how are we going to get in?"

Her mind raced. Surely there was something in this building that could be hacked? Some way to put a stop to the event inside. She had a phone and a laptop with her. She could trigger the fire alarm or the sprinklers or create some other havoc to get everyone evacuated.

But then, Cami thought again.

Perhaps she didn't even need to do that.

There might be a way for her to get inside, and all she would need would be herself. At any rate, it was worth a try.

"I've had an idea," she said to Connor. "Wait here, and let me see if it works. If it does, I'll go and open that fire door from the inside.

Cami removed her FBI hat and shook out her funky hairstyle.

Then she removed her FBI jacket, and she dug in her laptop bag and took out a black top, in loose knit, with silver threads running through it. It was trendy and ragged looking and was one of her most treasured garments.

She put it on over her T-shirt.

And then, hoping that her look and story would get her inside, she set off for the main door.

CHAPTER NINE

The doorman hadn't gotten a good look at her. That was what was on Cami's mind. She'd seen how he waved women through and clearly believed them to be no threat. And in any case, the narrow stairs had meant she was practically standing behind Connor. All he would have seen was her baseball cap and a glimpse of her uniform.

If she went back on her own, looking completely different, without that institutional uniform of the jacket and baseball cap, she didn't think he'd put two and two together since there was a steady stream of guests arriving. And her hairstyle wasn't what you'd expect from an FBI agent.

But she needed a cover story, too, and she had one prepared.

Tossing her hair back, lifting her chin, pushing up her sleeves to show off her tattoos, and slinging her laptop bag over her shoulder, Cami marched down the stairs to where the doorman was standing.

It didn't seem like he'd tried to warn Roland, and that was good. Perhaps that was overstepping his duties and they were limited to refusing police access.

"Hi," she said with a friendly smile.

"Can I help you?" he asked, frowning.

"I'm here for the sound mixing, for the Glamour Girls," she said in a matter-of-fact way.

"They've got someone already in there." He looked dubious.

"They need to leave. I got a message to come in and take over," Cami said, with a confident smile, as if she was used to doing this every working day.

She showed the doorman a completely fictitious incoming text on her phone, which she'd self-generated. But it looked authentic, it had a time and date, and a pin drop for the building.

"Okay," he said.

Her heart skipped a beat. Her cover story had held up, and she was going to get through the door.

He stepped aside, and Cami walked through the entrance, and found herself in the darkened depths of the Connoisseur's Club.

She heard the throb of music and the thud of the bass. This was more like a nightclub vibe than a smart function venue, she realized in surprise. Knowing she couldn't head directly to the fire exit to let Connor in, because the doorman might be watching, she headed into the main function area, where the music and action were booming out from. Perhaps she'd get a glimpse of Roland Coyne. Then they'd be able to move in on him quickly when Connor got in.

She took a breath, moving quietly through the darkened corridors, glowing with red lights and dancing spotlights. Her eyes were quickly adjusting from the bright sunlight outside to the dim interior, and she took a moment to look around.

Her feet trod on soft, plush carpet. She caught sight of herself in a large mirror on the wall.

This was definitely not a function venue, she realized in surprise. This was a major party destination. A waitress with a tray of drinks hustled past in the other direction. Above the music, she heard shouts and laughter.

The main area was huge, with tables and a dance floor in the center and alcoves on the side.

At the far side of the room, a small stage was bathed in soft, blue-white light, and two singers were performing, along with three scantily clad backup dancers.

In one of the alcoves, girls were dancing to the pounding beat of the dance track. In another, four men who looked in their early twenties were downing shots. From their raucous laughter and disheveled state, Cami guessed these were not their first shots of the night.

There were surely more than a hundred people here. This was no intimate client function. This was a full-on party with hordes of guests, and Cami guessed that if Roland was bringing clients here, it was so that they could all spend the afternoon and evening getting drunk—presumably on the company's dime.

"Hey, cutie!" The words came from behind her, and Cami turned. Three guys sprawled on a couch, with a bottle of champagne in front of them, were beckoning her over.

"Later, thanks," she said. It was time to get to the fire door and let Connor in.

Cami threaded her way through the crowds, heading for the steel door, walking quickly down the corridor so the doorman wouldn't notice her.

There was the fire door ahead. But there was a small problem. It was locked, with a key pad exit code.

Maybe there was an alternative exit through another section of what she was realizing was a far bigger place than it had looked from the outside. But for now, this was the exit where Connor would be waiting, and she needed to figure out how to open it.

A four-digit code should be easy to key in, as long as it was connected up to the building's wi-fi. And that would mean logging into the building's main system.

Plugging her phone into the laptop, she took shelter under a nearby table, so nobody would see what she was doing, and loaded the wi-fi hacking program. Sitting quietly in the dark, she hoped she'd be unobserved for the few minutes it took for the program to run.

She saw figures passing by from the main corridor, and her stomach tensed. She lowered the lid of her laptop, conscious that even though she was sure her dark clothing made her pretty much invisible, the glare of the screen might attract attention.

But to her relief, they didn't notice and passed by, talking and laughing to each other.

Cami hissed in a breath of frustration. The door wasn't hooked up to the main wi-fi at all. She could do a few other things. Turn on the sprinklers in different areas. Turn off the lights in different areas. But like the paper list, the stand-alone keypad was unhackable. It was too old-fashioned to be connected up.

She thought back to the reams of chit-chat on this exact topic that she'd had with fellow hackers. And she guessed that the only solution would be good, old-fashioned eyeballing of the keypad. If it was older—which she was guessing it was—perhaps the keys that formed the code were more worn.

Cami scrambled up, stepped forward, and looked closely at the keypad.

The number 1 was worn. So was the number 2. And the numbers 8 and 0 were worn.

She thought those were the correct digits, but there were still a massive number of permutations. She could be here a while trying them all, unless logic could get her a step further.

Who had originally decided on the code? Was it totally random or linked to something? Linked to something obvious would make it easier to open for everyone. Using someone's birthday wouldn't help everyone else.

Did it have anything to do with the phone number? She checked, but there were a few different numbers and she couldn't find a link there.

Cami was starting to panic. This door was defeating her, and Connor was waiting outside.

Maybe not the phone number, she thought suddenly. Maybe the street number. This club's address was 182 Cross Street. Therefore the zero might have been added at the end, to round the digits up to the necessary four.

Hoping that this would work because if it didn't, she was all out of ideas, Cami keyed in 1-8-2-0. She waited, feeling breathless.

The door buzzed, thinking about it for a few moments, and then, to her massive relief, it clicked open. She'd gotten it! Old-fashioned logic had helped her where modern methods hadn't been available. *Connor would be so proud,* she thought with a sudden flare of amusement.

Cami pulled the door open quickly. Connor was waiting outside.

"Good move, getting in by looking different," he said, striding in.

"We still have to find him," Cami said. "It's a big place, and I'm not sure where he is. I haven't seen him yet because I've been trying to figure out this door code."

"Let's go looking," Connor stated. Cami closed the door again, and they headed down the corridor.

"It is a big place. Like a maze," Connor said, raising his voice to be heard over the thump of the music. "Let's split up to search, and we text the other when we see him."

"Okay," Cami said. Feeling pleased to be playing more of an active role now, she headed inside, on the hunt.

Seeing Connor go to the left, Cami headed right, noticing a well-stocked bar ahead of her. The scent of alcohol was hanging in the air, together with a whiff of cigarette smoke. Where would Roland be? She had his face in her mind. He would be part of a group, she guessed. Entertaining clients. Although not in the way she'd expected, since this club was just an excuse for hard partying and drinking in a private setting. Maybe other stuff went on here. Maybe some of these pretty waitresses gave private dances, or there was drug use going on.

She looked into one of the alcoves, but couldn't see him there. There was a closed door beyond. Should she open it? Or would he be in the lounge area she could see beyond the bar? Deciding to try for the lounge area first, Cami headed there.

And then, she saw him.

He was sprawled on a couch, beer in hand, laughing at something being said by someone opposite him. It was the same guy, for sure. His dark good looks were distinctive and recognizable.

Quickly she messaged Connor, *"I found him. Lounge area, near the bar."*

But as she turned back, she saw to her worry that it didn't look like Roland was going to stay there for long. He was getting up, looking toward one of the passages that led into this labyrinth of rooms. Perhaps he had other clients to go and find. It seemed he was going to go deeper into the maze. It would be better to try and delay him, and without her hat and jacket, she'd have to use her charm. Such as it was, Cami acknowledged.

She sidled closer, wondering if she could get him into conversation. Luckily, it didn't seem as if it would be too difficult.

"Hey gorgeous," Roland slurred on seeing her, his eyes widening. "Love the hair."

"Hi," Cami smiled, trying her best to strike the "innocent but flirtatious" note.

Roland climbed unsteadily to his feet. She saw he was wearing a purple dress shirt and black suit pants. Perhaps he'd worn a tie earlier but now, his top button was undone. His face gleamed with a light sheen of perspiration, and she wondered if it was just excessive alcohol, or if he'd recently been dancing. His smile was confident.

"What are you doing here?"

"I'm here with a work colleague," Cami said, deciding to stick to being truthful.

"I'm also here for work. We come here a lot. Clients love it because it's so private and you can get up to all sorts of trouble. You want to come with me now? I'm going to the 'Inner Lounge.' One of the locked rooms on the floor below. I've got some nice stuff to share with you there."

Where was Connor, Cami wondered frantically. *He needs to get here. Now!*

"I'd love to come along with you. Let me just message my colleague and say where I'm headed. Can you wait?" She smiled. She didn't want him heading to a locked room. Or to be locked in a room with him.

He was getting impatient. The people he was sitting with had already gotten up and filtered away. Whatever the 'nice stuff' was, he clearly couldn't wait to get to it.

“Come on,” he said, smiling. He grabbed her arm and pulled her along in a half-coaxing, half-dominant way.

Cami felt panic flare. She needed him to stay here. Without a doubt, this man took what he wanted, and she wasn't sure of the right way to respond. She wanted to fight him off, but then she'd attract attention. And she sure couldn't let this go any further. She tried to wrench her arm away, but he held on.

“Come on,” he emphasized. “It’ll be fun.”

“You’re not letting me do what I need to!”

“Maybe I don’t want to.” There was a look in his eyes she didn’t like. She could see why he’d been trouble for Brooke. In a flash, he’d turned physical and forceful.

But at that moment, Connor strode over. Never had Cami been so relieved to see him arrive.

“What the—?” Astounded, Roland let go of her arm. Before Cami could blink, he had Roland's arm in a “friendly but not friendly” grip and was ushering him firmly out of the lounge.

“What are you doing, man?” Roland asked, sounding furious.

"FBI. I have some questions," Connor growled. "And I need answers."

"No way!" Now she saw panic in Roland's tone. "No way. I’m not talking to the police, man!"

Roland twisted his arm away. He shoved Connor fiercely, causing him to sprawl down on one knee.

And the next moment, he was racing across the carpet, heading for the dimly lit corridor beyond.

CHAPTER TEN

Cami felt horrified as Connor scrambled up, swearing, and set off in pursuit. He made a grab for Roland's arm and managed to snag his sleeve, but Roland turned, kicking out, showing an aggressive confidence that she hadn't expected from him.

He was big, strong, and fast. He got Connor in the knee—almost. At the last minute, Connor jumped back, swearing, as Roland turned and raced away. He was frighteningly quick, despite being so drunk. *Maybe that was because he was so drunk,* Cami thought, running after the two men.

At first, she thought he was going to storm right back into the main hall and most probably get help from one of the bouncers or doormen.

But then, as he reached the branch in the corridor, he hesitated. As if he was thinking things through.

And then he darted toward a side door, that Cami saw led to a steep, carpeted staircase.

He was going to flee downstairs to one of these locked rooms that he'd just bragged to her about. And if he went in there, it might be difficult to get him out. It would delay things. The club management and bouncers would get involved and they might now bring up the 'private property' argument to protect their own interests and guard their customers' privacy. Cami didn't know what the rules were in this situation, or if Connor might be forced to leave.

But suddenly she realized there was something she could do.

She'd logged into the wi-fi earlier, and although the fire door hadn't been on the system, there had been a lot of things that she had been able to control.

The lights!

That would work. He'd just bolted downstairs into the lower level. With Connor hot on his heels.

"I'm cutting the lights!" Cami called, hustling down the stairs, hoping he'd heard her.

Anxiety flared inside her as she realized she was up against the clock yet again. With shaking hands, she navigated the system. The lights were in different clusters.

Here was Lower Level 1 and Lower Level 2. This looked like 1, according to the layout.

Giving it a try, Cami stabbed the 'Off' button.

A complete and gratifying darkness descended.

From below, she heard a heavy, prolonged *thud* as if someone had tripped over his feet and fallen hard. She hoped it was Roland. Then, she heard the tramp of purposeful footsteps and the faint, dim glow of a light.

Following it, Cami headed downstairs.

Roland was lying on the carpet, groaning and breathing fast. Connor was on him, grabbing him firmly this time, with an arm twisted up behind his back, and his flashlight on the floor nearby.

As Cami watched, he pulled the other man to his feet.

Before everyone could come out of all the private lounges, Cami quickly reactivated the lights.

In their muted glow, Roland looked confused and angry. But now, with Connor hanging onto his arm with all his might and shoving him up against the carpeted wall, there was no more opportunity for him to break free.

Down here, the music was nothing more than a dull, subliminal thud. Their voices were audible—Connor's growl and Roland's angry protests.

"What are you doing? What the hell are you doing to me? This is oppression, man!"

"Unfortunately, you earned it," Connor said brusquely as he fastened the handcuffs around Roland's wrists.

"We have some questions," Connor pressured him.

"Questions?"

"First question, why did you run?"

"No reason. No reason at all." But Cami saw the instinctive guilt flare in his face. There was a reason, and she wondered what it might be. Perhaps he had a banned substance on his person. Maybe he was in possession of drugs. That would account for what he'd promised her as well. It had sounded like he was heading down here to do drugs.

But there could also be another reason, an even more important reason for Roland to want to avoid the police. And that was if he knew he'd committed serious crimes.

"Don't play cute with me, pal," Connor threatened.

"I was taken by surprise."

"By surprise?" Connor sounded deeply cynical.

Cami saw Roland's jaw clench. He started to say something and thought better of it. Instead, he clamped his mouth shut.

"We need the truth here. Starting now," Connor said sternly.

"I didn't do anything illegal," Roland said, sullenly.

"You just felt like some exercise suddenly?" Connor said.

"Look, you surprised me. I . . . I have issues with the cops, and I've been unfairly arrested in the past. I'm a little drunk now. As you can probably see. If you're going to come into a club and ask . . . ask members questions after having a few drinks, then you can't expect us to be as sober as we should be. Or act logically."

"We're investigating a murder."

Now, Roland's eyes widened. "A murder? You serious? Who's been killed?"

"Two women you're linked to."

"Me?" Roland's face went white. "Give me names, man. Without names this is all just a lot of . . . of hot air."

"Brooke Perkins. Cleo Booth."

Roland froze. His face had turned pale with shock, and he suddenly looked less drunk and more on the point of being sick.

"What?" he said. "Brooke?"

"You knew both women."

"I've no idea who Cleo is. I only know Brooke. She's murdered? Someone killed her?"

He did seem genuinely shaken, Cami decided. Was he that good of an actor? Or had he not known about Brooke's death?

She needed to be surer, and she thought she would be as Connor pressed on.

"Cleo wrote an expose article on your previous company, the one you worked for in Texas. It was very negative. It had destructive consequences. You must have known about it."

"I . . . I'm not even interested in that article. That firm was unfairly smeared. I know the back story. One partner who'd been involved in irregularities left and another ratted him out to the media. It was one of those things. I didn't even care who wrote the stupid piece, the blame was with the partners. I wasn't sorry to come back here. But now, I need to know about Brooke. What happened?"

Cami thought he now looked seriously stressed out.

"Her apartment was broken into, and she was deliberately targeted," Connor said calmly. "And as a result of that, we need to know your movements this morning. From seven a.m. to about nine a.m. Can you account for them?"

"Yes, yes I can do that," he stammered out. "I was at work. At the office. We had an early team meeting at eight. I arrived just after seven to prepare for it."

"Can you confirm that?"

"Can I confirm it?" Roland muttered the question, as if to himself. "Yeah, sure. I can confirm it."

"Go right ahead. We need details. And proof."

Cami thought that the shock of the last few minutes had gone a long way to sobering Roland up. Because he sounded more coherent as he answered.

"Sure. I called my secretary at seven-fifteen."

"From where? You could have called from the crime scene."

Roland glared at Connor. "She can confirm that I was at the office, in the conference room, briefing her on what to do and how to set the room out. She arrived at seven-thirty and found me working." He thought some more, his chest rising and falling hard. "There are cameras in the parking garage. If you need confirmation."

"We'll see what they tell us. Our office will be in touch to confirm that info," Connor said to him. "What about Tuesday? Where were you on Tuesday afternoon between the hours of five and six p.m.?"

That must have been when Cleo was murdered. Cami thought back to the details in the case file.

"Can I look on my phone?" Roland asked.

"Sure. If you're ready to share what you find straight away."

Connor unclipped one of the handcuffs, and Roland navigated to his online appointment diary, looking incoherent with stress.

"I was with a client," he said, sounding relieved.

"You were? Where? Here?" Connor sounded cynical.

"No. This was a meeting in the office. With one of our directors. I'll show you here. The meeting was from four till five-thirty, and then afterwards there were drinks and snacks brought in. We left at about seven. That's what happened. There are emails confirming it. And anyone at work can confirm we were there."

He turned his phone to show Connor.

Connor's lips tightened.

Cami could see that the evidence was, surprisingly, going to clear Roland. That wasn't what she'd expected. She now felt as shocked as he still looked. He'd had ties to both victims, and even reasons to want them dead, but he wasn't the killer.

Connor got on the phone to someone that Cami realized with a skip of her heart must be Ethan. Perhaps she'd get to see him soon. It sounded like Connor was instructing Ethan to check up on the details that still needed to be confirmed. But it sounded as if there was more to the conversation.

“You were about to call me?” he then asked, surprised, before continuing the conversation, but Cami couldn’t pick up much from the one-sided “Yes,” “No,” and “Where?”

And then, Connor got off the phone, his face grim.

"You can go," he told Roland, who turned and stumbled away, still looking shell shocked from what had played out.

To Cami, he said, "Ethan was able to confirm enough to clear him from a quick call to the office. But we have to go. We have new information that just landed, and it could be important."

CHAPTER ELEVEN

Cami hustled out of the Connoisseur's Club, hot on Connor's heels. New information? Where had it come from, and what did it mean for the case?

Connor strode out the main door, with the doorman giving him an astonished look, as if putting two and two together too late, and wondering how on earth he'd gotten in. Cami followed close behind, hustling past before the doorman could start asking anything more.

"We have to go to the pathology offices," Connor said, when they were back on the street and heading to the car. "They've picked up a common factor in the postmortems of the two women, and they want us to see it."

Cami stopped in her tracks on hearing that. But seeing Connor was powering on, she had no choice but to follow. Now, though, her stomach was churning.

She thought that she would be able to avoid the stark sight of bodies this time around. But now, it seemed like she wouldn't.

There was going to be no negotiation here. That she knew. If Connor was going to the pathology lab, there was a valid reason for it, and all she could do was to follow behind and hope that she managed to cope with what lay ahead.

Dead bodies were deeply distressing to her, because they reminded her too strongly of what had gone on in her mind after Jenna had disappeared, where all her worst fears had surged. Cami had had sleepless nights, many of them, imagining what might have happened to her sister. She knew there was a reason why she'd gone, and that she had not just run away. She wouldn't have run away. Cami had played and replayed their recent conversations, their late night whispered chats. In none of them had Jenna so much as hinted that she would be leaving suddenly.

The potential violent scenarios that could have played out had given Cami terrible nightmares. And she'd never gotten over the fear of what her big sister, who'd always shielded and protected her, might have suffered. The autopsy tables brought all those thoughts to terrible reality.

But she knew that Connor was prickly and critical about her behavior in these environments. And equal to her trauma, Cami found, was her pride in standing up for herself.

She did not want Connor to see her breaking down, throwing up, or refusing to go into the room. That was not an option. She would do anything to avoid it.

So, there was no other choice but to tread into that room on leaden feet and try to dissociate herself from the horrors it held.

***

The autopsy room was quiet, late into the evening and heading toward night. There was only one person at the reception desk, and a scattering of staff in the building, which Cami noted was uncomfortably cold, the same as last time.

It smelled of disinfectant, with an undertone of other odors that she didn't want to think about.

Even though there was a skeleton staff on duty after hours, they were busy checking in at the desk when a commotion sounded outside, and a gurney was wheeled hastily in by two paramedics. Their uniforms were streaked and spattered with dirt and blood. They veered quickly in the direction of one of the right hand autopsy rooms, waved over urgently by a waiting pathologist.

Cami watched, feeling as if she was descending too fast in an out of control elevator.

"Who's the doc on duty?" Connor asked the attendant at the reception desk. "We're here to see the autopsies on Perkins and Booth."

"That'll be Doc Farah," the woman replied, pointing the opposite way from where the incoming gurney had gone. She didn’t know Doctor Farah. They had dealt with a different doctor last time. There wasn’t going to be any hint of familiarity in this stark and unforgiving space.

She saw Connor give her an odd glance.

"This is important," he muttered. "Keep alert. Pick up what we need."

"I will," she muttered back, feeling nausea surge as he led her over to where the masks and gloves awaited.

Cami gowned up as a tall man, whose features she couldn't even see clearly behind his mask and eyeglasses, came out of the nearest room.

"Connor," he said.

"Farah," Connor replied, clearly familiar with this pathologist.

"I've got something to show you. We suspected it after the first autopsy. But this one made it more likely. However, we're not a hundred percent sure yet. I'd like your take on it."

"Let's have a look."

Even though Connor's face was now swathed in a mask, Cami could see his eyes were bright and alert. She wondered if he'd ever felt the same as her when confronted by a corpse on a slab. Maybe long ago when he'd started out, but not for years, certainly. Now, her supervisor and partner had been able to wall off the horror and focus only on what was going to get the case further.

Maybe she'd be able to do that, too, one day. Especially if a year's involvement now awaited her.

She felt apprehensive, but determined to fight her fear, as she walked into the chilly room, and her chest tightened as she saw the two sheet-swathed figures on the metal tables. They seemed so vulnerable, so small in death. Struggling to get a handle on her stomach churning nausea, Cami now added sadness to her stew of emotions as she glanced at them.

The doctor strode straight over to the closest one and pulled back the sheet. Instinctively, Cami dropped her gaze to the floor. *Damn,* she thought. She hadn't wanted to do that, but this was sheer survival.

"Now, as you can see, the knife strokes in the two victims are clearly from the same, or a very similar, weapon. They slice deep into the back. It's probably the second out of three that killed her. The first was too high, and by the third, she was already collapsing."

"Yes, I see," Connor said, sounding fascinated.

"But what we did note was the angle of the cuts. Now it was hard to tell here. But take a look at the second victim. This time, there were four strokes. Probably also the second was a fatal blow, as was the third, because she took longer to fall."

"Yes," Connor said.

"But you see the angle here?"

She heard his voice, sharp and intense, like a knife itself.

"Left handed?" he said.

Cami's head jerked up.

That was important. That would narrow down the identity of the killer substantially.

"We can't be sure. And also, there's the chance that he simply favors that hand for physical activity, and the other is still dominant. But it's something to look out for," the doctor emphasized.

"Wait a minute." Cami heard her voice, shaky but loud enough for both Connor and Farah to look around.

"I might be able to confirm that," she said. "From the camera footage."

The footage she had on her phone. From the security camera in Brooke's apartment lobby.

She'd looked at where the killer buzzed himself in. She'd seen which button he'd pressed. But she hadn't noticed which hand he'd used, and now, combined with this other evidence, it was suddenly critical.

She rewound the footage. She looked again.

"Left," she said, feeling all the more triumphant that she'd managed to do this while in the stressful environment of the autopsy room. "Take a look." She turned the phone their way. Without a doubt, their killer had raised his left hand to the buzzer, unerringly.

"Left handed for sure. That narrows it down." Connor turned to the pathologist. "Thanks. You've given us a good lead. And thanks for confirming it," he told Cami.

To Cami's relief, they then left the autopsy room. The night air on her perspiring face felt cool and fresh as they headed back to the car.

"What are we doing now?" she asked Connor.

"Well, exploring direct contacts hasn't worked so far, but I'm going to keep following up on it in case there are others we haven't yet pinpointed. But I have a different job for you." He glanced at her.

"What's that?" she asked.

"These victims were both very active online. They were both vocal and outspoken. So that's where we need to look for connections now. We now need to find out if they had any opponents or critics in common. Someone might have become aware of them online, didn't like what they had to say, and might have decided to silence them both. If such a person exists, we need to find him."

CHAPTER TWELVE

The tracker was following the attractive brunette woman online, watching as she commented on a general interest social media group. It was a pet ownership group. *You would think such a group would be fun and harmonious,* he thought. But she could take conflict with her anywhere. In fact, she seemed hell bent on pushing her views across and getting into fights.

He wasn't missing a nuance. One browser was open, tracking her words and her actions. Even her thoughts, he decided, as he hunched over the screen, narrowing his eyes as he waited for her words to appear.

This was one of the women he loathed, and her name was Emma Pratley. He had known about her for a few weeks. He had hated her ever since he'd seen her comment.

Emma Pratley was now in a debate with another woman. He felt filled with anger as he saw the interaction play out.

"The truth is black and white, you do know that. So maybe you should stop trying to justify yourself when you're wrong. Stop trying to explain a load of trash about kids in daycare?" Emma Pratley's expression, the sharp tone of her voice, the heavy sarcasm—all were anathema to him. He resented this woman and what she stood for.

"You're just bullying me! Why can't you accept alternative points of view that are actually concerned about responsible parenting?"

"Your point of view is not alternative. It's blindingly incorrect. You need to learn some logic, or maybe some intelligence, because you're not impressing me with anything so far. You're just getting over-emotional."

In fact, this other woman in this debate with Emma Pratley had seemed to value calmness and rationality, but was clearly no match for Emma Pratley's superior, aggressive debating tactics. She couldn't handle the levels of abuse, and she was becoming visibly upset.

"You're gaslighting! You're being totally unfair, and I resent your personal insults," her opponent retorted.

"And why's that? Does the truth hurt? The truth is that you don't know a thing about your topic, and you're talking out of pure ignorance." Emma shot back.

"We moved away from truth a long time in this argument. You're just trying to be destructive!"

He could see she was getting angry, triggered by the subtle needling and the superior stance that Emma Pratley was deliberately taking. This was all intentional. He knew that Emma didn't care about logic herself. Most likely, she didn't really care about responsible parenting either, especially since she wasn't a parent herself. She just wanted to win, even though it meant causing rage, anger, and making people upset. It was almost as if Emma Pratley was feeding off this negative emotion.

"Calm down. Why are you getting so worked up? Can't you handle debate?" Emma pressed on.

"This is not debate. You're cyberbullying," her opponent replied.

He could see that the interaction had triggered an emotional response, causing Emma Pratley to press home her advantage even further in a gleefully superior way. It was all a crude form of manipulation.

"If you can't take the heat, stay out of the kitchen," Emma Pratley wrote in a condescending tone. *"That's what online is all about. Or is this your first day on the internet, Momsie?"*

He hated this savage and voracious woman. She was insatiable, grasping for spoils at any cost. He was enraged by what he saw. He slammed his fist on the table so hard that it shook.

But deep inside, the logical part of his mind was still working and observing.

He saw that Emma Pratley liked to spend a long time online. She never quit an argument when she was embroiled in one. Thirty to sixty minutes, at least, was the time she spent trying to destroy and belittle her opponents. Because she was brutally direct, she always stirred up a storm. If one opponent dropped out, others replaced him or her. And there was always a worrying level of support for Emma herself, despite her vicious tactics. People often stood up for the bully and liked to see others destroyed. He was sure that made her feel gleeful and victorious.

But tactics aside, her timing was important to him, because he needed to know the window of opportunity that he would have.

Now, he saw it meant he could make her pattern work for him, and deliver his message precisely when she was there to receive it. It might even be possible tonight. The next few minutes would tell.

He felt a thrill of excitement and anticipation rising within him. He knew what he needed to do now. He would need to time his approach so that he could catch her at a moment when she was alone and online.

He moved to the other tabs. They were his dossier of information, his personal storage facility.

He knew that when they met, when he came face to face with Emma for the first time, it had to be perfect. His plans had to roll out seamlessly, as foolproof as any plan could be in this world where there was so much room for error and complication.

His dossier on her was carefully compiled to ensure that there would be no room for error. He even had the plans for her building, which he'd discovered online. There were some details there that would help him. A lucky find, but he was the first to admit that you made your own luck in this world.

Counting off on his fingers, he listed the information he had.

"Plans," he said aloud, his voice hoarse, because he hadn't spoken for a few hours in this solitary perusal of the online world. "Map. Address. She's a Boston girl. Timing. Neighbors. And I know exactly who she is and what she looks like."

He'd done his work there, for sure. He knew this woman lived in a small, double-story house that she shared with another professional woman. But the other woman regularly travelled overseas for work. She'd just left and would be in London for the next week.

That meant Emma Pratley would be alone. The home to her right was occupied by a family with three young children. He'd spent time studying their comings and goings because that was a potential unknown. He had a good idea of their schedule now. In the evening, they were locked up tight. The exhausted parents never seemed to go out, and he had a feeling that there would be so much noise and activity in the house at night that they wouldn't take much notice of anything happening outside.

On the other side was a couple who worked until late and often socialized. They were seldom home until late, especially toward the end of the week, Thursday through Saturday. So they, too, would be accounted for.

This left Emma Pratley alone in her house, at a moment when there would be no witnesses, no concerned neighbors to interfere with his plans.

He had all the details he needed. It was perfect, like a dream come true. From the plans, he was sure he could get in through the back door.

He knew what it looked like, where the door and windows were. He knew what the fencing was like, and that it was easy to climb. He was also aware of the cameras in the area. This being a peaceful, middle income suburban area, there were very few. None of the residents nearby, including Emma, had camera security in place in their own homes. She had an alarm, that he knew, but it was only activated when she went out.

And he planned to meet with her when she was in.

He smiled at the thought. He was relishing the moment, looking forward to the time—those brief few seconds—where she would realize she'd gone too far, crossed a line, and the consequences had come her way. He loved the thought of that moment. It was justice—pure, simple, and undiluted. In its finest form. Retribution that he, and he alone, could bring.

It was time to go.

If he moved fast, then his work could get done tonight. What a bonus that would be. It seemed as if circumstances were in his favor and he would soon be able to do what he needed to do, once again.

Standing up, with a cold grin on his face, the tracker shut down his screens and left, walking swiftly out into the night.

CHAPTER THIRTEEN

Somewhere out in this darkened city, a man might be watching and listening online, shadowing people's comments, picking his targets, and moving in for the physical kill. *Was there such a man,* Cami wondered, *and if so, how could she root him out from the online world where he hid?*

She headed into the FBI offices, walking shoulder to shoulder with Connor, her mind racing ahead as she thought about the best ways to track him down.

They headed straight up to Connor's offices. Cami was impressed by the fact that this building truly never seemed to sleep. Even now, well after office hours, there was a buzz of activity from behind the doors they passed. The elevators were riding up and down nonstop, and they had to wait for one to be available and then stand aside so that three stressed-looking agents could walk out. Talking in low voices, the trio hurried to the exit, most definitely on a work mission and not heading home.

Cami opened her laptop even before she sat down, and as soon as she was perched on Connor's office chair, she began putting together her ideas.

"Firstly, I'm going to look at what these victims said and did while online," she told Connor. “That might give us a clue about who targeted them.”

"So you're going to assess their personas, the impression they gave?" he asked.

"Yes."

"When you have that information, pass it over to me. I can help there," he said. "Sourcing it is not my strong suit. But reading into it is. It might also help me with looking into their real lives more closely.”

"That'll be great. I'll do that," she said.

"And then?" he asked.

"Then I'm going to see if there are any opponents that they triggered. Perhaps there was a direct confrontation with someone that escalated, and there might still be a record of that where it happened.

I’ll need to know what their stamping grounds are, where they interacted."

“In my experience, when people get angry enough to have physical confrontations after arguing online, it can go two ways,” Connor said.

"What are those?" Cami asked.

"Either they back down and end up being decent people, apologize, and start being polite and reasonable again. Or else it goes the opposite way and the conflict escalates radically."

"To violence?"

"Yes. To serious violence. It's happened before. We have case history of kidnappings, assault, and even murder that's occurred after fights have escalated online. The FBI doesn't always get involved as some crimes don't fall within our jurisdiction, but we do keep up to date with the serious crimes in our areas."

"How common is that?"

"It's rare, but there is a clear case precedent. Even if comments were deleted afterward. But most times, people seem to think that their online transactions have no relevance to what they did in the real world. It’s strange how someone can literally go out and egg someone’s house or beat someone up while leaving all the evidence online."

Hoping that she’d get a similar lucky break, Cami set out to discover what these victims really had been getting up to, and what enemies they had made in their online world.

First prize, she knew, would be if the two women had an adversary in common. Someone who’d threatened both of them, or else someone who’d just ended up in an argument with both. Either scenario might be correct. But she wasn’t so sure about leaving a clear trail of tracks to follow. After all, this killer had gotten in and out of the houses with such speed and precision. He was sneaky and stealthy. For sure, he was a planner.

So, she would need to be sneaky too. She'd need to look out for subtle signs and indications. She wasn't sure what they would be.

But as she took a look online at the sites, groups, and social media platforms where these women had spent their time, Cami found—to her surprise—that she was developing strong opinions about them.

“I hate to have to say this,” she said, and then stopped, feeling bad about continuing.

“Say what?” he prodded her.

"These women weren't nice!" she admitted to Connor. "I'm going to forward you some conversation threads to show you what I mean. It feels wrong to criticize them, because they're dead, but you can see how they made enemies online. They were both . . . opinionated when they were feeling in a good mood. But trolls, I guess you'd call them, when they were in a bad mood. Real life trolls." Cami felt terrible saying such a thing, but facts were facts. They'd acted appallingly in some of the threads she was reading. It was as if they had deliberately fomented anger and conflict and then fed on the fallout.

"These are adults, presumably well-educated, but they have been saying things online that most people wouldn't dream of saying in public. I know online is not always anonymous, but maybe being in front of a screen instead of face to face with somebody made them feel—I guess, insulated from the consequences."

"That, we've seen a lot of," Connor admitted. "As have the police. Online bullying is an epidemic and as you say that dissociation between real life and the screen makes people think it's okay."

"I can't believe Cleo or Brooke would be so aggressive in person. No way," Cami said.

"It seems their behavior could have provided a reason for what happened," Connor said thoughtfully, reading through the conversation snippets that Cami was sending. "What I am noticing though is that their profiles are very closed. Very private."

"Yes. They don't give much information out, and that means that the killer must have found another way to work out who they were. I mean, Cleo's profile doesn't even state she lives in Boston. It says 'Journalist: National Issues'. Brooke is on a few community groups, so it makes it more likely. But why were they targeted, apart from their atrocious behavior? Why them?"

"And who else?" Connor said.

He sighed heavily, and Cami knew he was thinking of the next crime. Would there be a third? Was this killer stalking someone he perceived to be doing wrong right now?

As she read through the baiting, the insults, and the vicious interactions that both women had taken part in, she could see how someone might have been triggered to take action in real life and to kill.

Being bitchy online was no excuse for murdering someone. But for someone damaged, someone psychopathic, someone who had experienced some kind of psychotic break—then yes, it might have flipped the switch they needed.

"Well, let's find the connection, Cami," she muttered to herself. "Then we can work on where this person might be, and what he's up to now."

She worked through the conversations, noting down names, highlighting interactions, looking for the red flags that showed themselves as she speed-read through the conversations. Cami found herself checking time stamps, noting the reactions to the comments, trying to work back and figure out if there were any gaps or referrals that might mean a comment had been deleted.

"You know, I think I'm picking something up here," she said.

There was a man who was a lurker on a few of the political sites and the Boston-based community sites. His name was Peter Frost. He was a Boston local, and he hadn't commented often. But she found a comment saying "Peter, don't threaten her. It's a valid point."

The "her" in question was Brooke. And the threat seemed to have been removed. That comment was no longer visible, only the response to it.

That was interesting.

Now, had Peter had any interaction with Cleo?

She went quickly and looked on Cleo's most favored sites, hoping that she could find a connection.

And as she read down the threads, her eyes narrowed. There was something here.

A definite threat. Not deleted. Still there. And strong enough for Cleo to have backed off of her bullying.

"I'm going to make sure you regret it if you carry on this way. Cyberbullying is a crime, and crimes deserve punishment," Peter had written.

So was murder. Murder was a crime too. Had Peter gone one step further and decided to silence Cleo and Brooke permanently for their perceived bullying tactics? It was time to find out.

CHAPTER FOURTEEN

It was time to make his move. The tracker was no longer operating in the online matrix. He had migrated to the real world. Just as it had been for him the past two times, he found the intensity of the thoughts and feelings overpowering as he waited in the car, a block or two away, silent, hidden, and unseen.

His breath was rapid, and his hands were cold. But his mind was focused.

He'd done this the first time out of an overriding need, a compulsion. It had passed in a blur and he hadn't even been fully aware of each moment.

He'd been so tense. So fraught with emotion.

And yet, so cold. So ordered in his thinking, despite his feelings.

It was strange, he thought. Almost as if there was a dissociation between the two. That his mind was actually splitting in two. The emotional side and the cold, implacable side. That was how it felt to him.

He could remember Brooke's expression before she'd turned and run, and Cleo's eyes growing wider and wider with each step he took toward her before she, too, had broken and fled. But nothing about the memories made him feel any regret. Rather, he felt a cool satisfaction that they had gotten what they deserved.

The second kill he'd made had been easier. Time seemed to slow down. The details became more vivid. Rather than feeling a compulsion to get it over without being seen, he had wished for more time to enjoy the satisfaction of the payback he was meting out.

He was gaining confidence and expertise, he guessed, and that was just as well. Because there were many more people who needed the same punishment. Luckily, he had the expertise and the specific skills needed to find out who those people were, even when they tried to hide away behind closed, private identities. There was a huge satisfaction in achieving this.

He thought about that as he paced slowly down the road.

His blade was well hidden, deep in a pocket of his jacket. His head was bowed as if in thought or tiredness. He knew where the cameras were. Here was one—one of the few—outside a small restaurant. He crossed the road to avoid it, because he didn't want to be captured on the footage if there was a choice.

Last time, there hadn't been a choice, and so he had wrapped up, obscured his face as best he could, and opted for a brutal, fast entry.

He would be fast this time, too, and yet there was no reason for anyone to suspect him.

He still looked like a decent, ordinary citizen in his carefully chosen outfit and his innocent looking shiny shoes. Just an innocent guy, going home late from work. That was his cover story this time, and to make sure it held up, he had a briefcase in his hand.

It was a nice neighborhood, too, he noticed as he glanced around as he strode. It confirmed in real life what he'd seen online. Neat yards, well-maintained trees, and a feeling of peace and quiet.

That would soon be shattered thanks to him. But then again, all he was doing was ensuring payback.

The fault lay with those who had chosen to do what they did. They were begging for death in their choices. They had thrown stones at someone else's life. Now it was their turn to suffer.

I am just the messenger, he thought, with a small, cold smile that felt strange on his face.

A woman passing by, walking a dog, gave him a quick nod of greeting, which he returned politely. But her gaze immediately slid away, and he felt a flare of relief. She saw no threat in him and would probably not remember him. His briefcase gave him the cover he needed, and that single, businesslike prop was enough to convince people of his credentials.

He was cold, calm, and focused. This time, he intended to enjoy the moment when he took her. This time, he was going to savor the confrontation.

An image of each of the women flashed across his mind's eye. And the need for payback burned hot inside him.

Abruptly, his emotions flared again. Fury seethed, like nothing he'd felt before. The desire for justice was an overwhelming thing inside him.

He took a deep breath and exhaled.

If his targets had not been so nasty and had not driven others to tears and distress, then they would not have ended up on his list. But they had, they had chosen that outcome. And he was the one who could bring them everything they deserved.

He felt a burst of excitement as he turned into Emma's driveway and saw the house. The curtains were closed, with a glow of light filtering from inside. The light was on in the lounge, and he guessed that was where she was now, no doubt with her phone or laptop on her knee. Sprinklers were on in the front yard, sending water arcing into the flower beds.

He checked, looking on his phone quickly to make sure she was online, and on the site he'd predicted, hunched over her phone or laptop, causing mayhem and conflict.

Sure enough, she was. Immediately, he saw that his new target was busy on a local group that had become embroiled in the discussion—ironically—of whether more street cameras should be put up in the wider suburb. There was hot debate for and against. Those wanting the cameras were obviously the proponents of safety. Those against were complaining about the cost and the lack of privacy. Both arguments were valid, he saw merit in both points of view as long as both were courteously debated, of course.

He himself was able to respect other views even though for him personally, no cameras was the better outcome. But his target was not, and she was running rampant now. That was what these women lacked. Respect. He'd watched it again and again, and he was seeing it now.

The group numbered in the thousands and he'd joined a few days ago. He'd lurked and bided his time since then.

He doubted she cared either way about the cameras, but she was taking an opposing stance to one of the others, and was playing her usual game. Taunting. Baiting. Being insulting and getting personal, while adroitly putting the blame on her opponent for being "emotional" and "unreasonable." It was a skilled attack and a hard one to counter.

Luckily, he was now going to be able to counter it in person. He pulled on his gloves and strode swiftly up to the door. This was the time he had waited for. The time to make sure every step of his plan was correctly done.

He had a few tools in the briefcase. He knew a little about DIY, and when you broke into a house, you didn't need a huge crowbar, you just needed the basics, and to apply pressure in the correct place.

With a hard shove he did just that, and the lock capitulated, splintering inward.

She'd know he was there now, and that was fine. She wouldn't get out in time. She'd probably run, and that was also okay. He knew exactly where to stab in the back. He'd researched it thoroughly, practiced it before he'd headed out for the first time. In the back was ideal because there was something poetic about it. In his opinion these online bullies were all backstabbers themselves.

His blade was stiletto sharp.

Knowing he would see the fear in her eyes, he burst inside, moving fast. Now it was all about speed and resolve. For this moment, he found it helpful to think of her not as a person, but as a thing of evil that needed to be brought down. He strode through the hall, his footsteps loud, and turned into the lounge where he was certain he'd find her.

In just a minute, he knew, he would be typing those words onto the online group. In caps. "I'M DEAD. GOODBYE."

He couldn't wait for that moment.

And there she was, her eyes widening as she saw him, her phone falling to the ground, thudding down on the carpet as she scrambled to her feet.

"No!" she screamed. "No!"

She turned and ran. It was the last thing she did.

CHAPTER FIFTEEN

It was late, but Cami barely noticed the time ticking by as she followed the trail to this man's online identity. Who was this person who had threatened both women, and more importantly, why did he feel safe voicing such blatant threats online?

"His real name's not Peter Frost," she said. That was why.

"He's got a fake account?" Connor asked.

"Yes. He must have thought he was anonymous and safe in making those threats?" she suggested.

"So who is he really?" Now Connor sounded impatient.

The problem was that his real identity seemed to be very well hidden.

"I'm looking. I'm looking," Cami said, moving from her phone to the four different tabs she now had open on her laptop. "He's hiding away, but I'm going to find him."

Connor looked pointedly at the digital clock on his desk, as the numbers slid from 9:02 p.m. to 9:03 p.m. It was getting late, but she'd never felt less tired in her life. *Connor looked tired,* she thought, and his face was showing his age, but he was soldiering on as if tiredness was an all too familiar companion on these cases. It would take more than the weight of a few decades on this earth to derail his focus.

All she needed to do was to find one link. There was always a link, right?

"There's always a link," she said aloud.

"Is there always?" Connor said, and now she could hear that he sounded doubtful.

"There always is. It's not always easy to find, but people are careless sometimes, and even if they aren't, there are ways to match it up. I'm running a couple of programs here."

She had two different programs on the go, and was also physically searching through any records she could. Including the hidden records that most people didn't access. Cami could get to some of them. She had backdoor programs that could run. These were written by expert hackers, and they were done as reverse insurance policies for those who needed to have seriously well-hidden identities that could not be found.

She ran search algorithms on each data set, but still nothing popped out. She'd come up dry.

Cami redefined the parameters of her search with a new set of data. She was going to make the assumption that this killer lived in, or near, Boston. She thought he was a local. She didn't think he would have traveled out of state to a different city and killed with such ease and speed. It was her bet that he'd been living here a while and doing research online and also, somehow, in person.

Of course, she could be wrong, but it was at least a place to start. And with those parameters, she picked up what she needed to.

"I've got him!" she said triumphantly, as Connor crowded over.

"Who is he?" he asked eagerly.

"His real name is Samuel Nolan. He's been living in Boston since he was in his early twenties," she announced, pointing to his address. "He's thirty-seven years old."

"And what does Mr. Nolan do for a living?"

Connor was already turning to his own screen, and Cami guessed that he was going to run a search on the name and see if there was any criminal record linked to it. Perhaps Samuel Nolan had slipped up in the past.

"He's a creepy character!" Cami said, sounding surprised. "I can't believe what I'm reading here."

"What?" Connor hurried over once more, abandoning his own search to breathe down her neck again.

Turning the screen, she showed him what she had finally found.

"He's a local filmmaker. A small scale guy. He shoots indie films, commercials, local events, that sort of thing. But a while ago—in fact, just a couple of months back, he did something different."

She flicked to the incriminating screen, and heard Connor's breath hiss in.

"Wow," he said.

"I know, right?"

Cami couldn't believe her eyes as she read through the summary of the short movie—a personal venture—that Nolan had recently shot and produced.

"*Troll Hunter,* it's called," she said aloud. "And it's basically a revenge fantasy movie about someone who gets his own payback on online trolls."

"That's exactly what seems to be playing out here," Connor said.

"*Troll Hunter* is the short film everyone who's ever been bullied online needs to watch," Cami read, feeling more and more fascinated by the similarities between this movie and the killer they were hunting. "*Troll Hunter* takes us through a day in the life of a man who turns to murder in real life to do what he's always longed to—to take down the trolls, bullies, and fakes that inhabit the cyber world. This gritty movie, shot in an urban fantasy setting and featuring an enigmatic 'cyber' hero, has made a profit of fifty thousand dollars since its release. *Troll Hunter* is a commercial success and a movie for today's modern viewer. Dark and violent, it takes some guts to watch it, but for sure, it's won the glory."

"Is that a review?"

"Yes, that's the intro. And here's Nolan."

She turned the screen to show a photo of the filmmaker. He looked just as she would have expected a man to look who'd dreamed up a revenge movie plot and then followed it up with real life kills. He had a high forehead, a hooked nose, and dark, brooding eyebrows. He looked like a medieval torture chamber assistant dragged into the modern world.

"Where does he live?" Connor was focusing on the practical side, less captivated by this man's appearance. At that moment, his own search engine pinged.

"Wait a minute!" He rushed back to his screen. "Information came in from the archives. Nolan has a record of assault. Two years ago, he was given a suspended sentence after attacking a man who made derogatory comments online about one of his movies."

"So, that could be where he started and escalated afterward?" Cami was feeling like a hound that had caught the scent. This exhausting and arduous research had finally paid off, and it had led them to a man who was checking all the boxes they needed to identify the killer.

"I've got his home address here," Connor said.

"Wait a minute. I'm finding something else also," Cami said. There was a fragment of information she'd spotted that she thought would prove useful. "He rents a studio in the warehouse area. And it says here they're currently filming *Beyond Night*—a revenge thriller with a twist. There's a time schedule here and it looks as if filming is still in progress. So, I'm wondering if we should go straight there?"

"Let's go to the studio first," Connor decided. "If we don't catch him at work, he'll be home, but if the schedule says he's still filming, I've never known a movie crew to wrap up early."

Cami grabbed her bag, and they headed out.

If she was right, then in fifteen minutes, they would be face to face with the killer.

CHAPTER SIXTEEN

Fifteen minutes later, Cami and Connor pulled up outside the warehouses. This was a perfect destination for a dark-minded suspect, she decided. The warehouses were shadowy and almost deserted. The building they wanted—number four—had a dim light flickering outside, and the door was firmly closed.

Connor knocked.

There was no reply from inside.

He knocked again, louder.

And then, the door was pulled open, and he came face to face with a woman in garish make-up. Her face was deathly white, and she had fake blood oozing down her left cheek. Despite herself, Cami flinched at seeing a bloodied corpse in the doorway.

"What is it?" she asked, surprised to see them. "We've got all the necessary permits in place."

"This isn't about permits," Connor said. He grasped the door and opened it wider, so that she stepped back, and he was inside. *Cleverly done,* Cami thought. He'd gained access to the property before she could refuse it. "I'm FBI Special Agent Connor, and it's in connection with murder cases. We're looking to speak to Mr. Nolan."

From the door ahead, which was open a crack, Cami could hear weird, moaning music. Filming was clearly in progress, and she was sure he must be in there. The woman looked unsure.

"Look, he's through there, but—" she began.

Thank you," Connor said.

He marched to the door and opened it wide.

Cami gasped. With a green screen background, a man dressed in a ragged black robe was lifting a gleaming knife high as a woman cowered away. The music crescendoed. The knife came down, a slick, shiny weapon of death.

And then a voice yelled, "Cut!"

A short, blond haired man turned and hurried over to them, with an annoyed expression on his face.

"We're filming. That was a take, and we're going to have to redo it. What is it? What do you want?"

"FBI. We need to ask some questions in connection with a murder," Connor said. "We're looking for Mr. Nolan."

The man's face went very still for a moment.

"Mr. Nolan?" he repeated loudly.

"Correct," Connor said.

"He's . . . he's not here," the man stammered but Cami was sure he was lying.

"Not here? This is a movie shoot, and he's the director?"

"I'm managing this scene," the man said firmly. "If you want to speak to him, you'll need to come back."

"I think you're lying to us. Do you know there are consequences for lying to law enforcement?" Connor threatened.

But Cami, as she watched and replayed that scene in her mind, had realized something.

The lead actor had only turned his face to them for a moment, but his features had looked remarkably like Nolan's. He wasn't directing, because he was in the movie, playing a starring role as the killer.

Now, as she looked at the screen, she saw that he was no longer there. He'd run for it. He'd fled the scene with a knife in his hand.

In his left hand, Cami now realized with a clench of her stomach. That might mean he was, in fact, left-handed. And now, they needed to find him before he got away completely.

"Get the lights on! Get that man back here!" Cami heard Connor bellow as he ran. He pounded through the warehouse in pursuit of the fleeing suspect.

But Cami was sure that Nolan was no longer there and could not hear the words. She was sure he'd snuck out of a door and was even now fleeing through the darkened streets beyond.

Nobody else did anything as they ran past. The actress and cameramen just stared, frozen in shock, as Connor sped through the scene, heading to the area behind the green screen where Nolan had melted away.

Connor was chasing him surprisingly fast, Cami saw. She hadn't expected that this tall, solid agent in his fifties could actually move like lightning. It was taking everything she had to keep up.

She followed Connor, racing to a door she now saw behind the green screen area. This was where he'd bolted to. For sure, he was out now, running in the dark.

Connor burst through the door, and Cami followed.

The door opened onto a narrow back road with a damp, potholed strip of blacktop cutting between the bulk of the warehouses. It was dark, filled with shadows and silence. Where had he gone?

Connor hesitated, breathing hard, looking from side to side. Cami guessed he was using all his senses to try and locate this suspect.

"You stay with me," he muttered to Cami. "Guy's got a knife, and we don't want any heroics going wrong."

Cami felt a strange mix of relief and inadequacy. She wanted to help, to be proactive, to get out there and chase after this suspect on her own, and not be a burden to Connor. She could see how two trained agents could split up, left and right, covering both directions on this narrow road, bringing the chances of catching this suspect close to one hundred percent.

But at the same time, she knew she didn't have the skills to cope with such a chase down.

He had a knife. He might already have killed with it, and she didn't know how to defend herself. And that meant she would be tagging along behind Connor and their chances were all the way down to fifty percent or less.

Was there any way of figuring out where he'd gone? She couldn't see any footprints or any indication. Both directions looked equally unappealing.

He must know the area. So perhaps he had somewhere in mind. Could he have gone into another warehouse? She didn't think so. Everything looked securely locked up at this hour.

Deciding on the left, with a frustrated shrug, Connor began jogging along the blacktop, pulling a flashlight off his belt. The beam didn't go a very long way in banishing the shadows and darkness that lurked in every corner. Cami's eyes strained as she jogged behind him.

There was something! Her eyes spotted movement, and her head whipped around. But it was nothing more than the flutter of a black trash bag, abandoned in the corner and now ruffled by the cool breeze that was being channeled down this narrow road.

Her ears strained for the sound of breath, footsteps, or any sign of his presence. But there was nothing.

"Look," Connor whispered and Cami saw something further on.

It was an opening under the awning of another warehouse, that seemed to lead off to the left. He turned toward it, and they both ran closer.

Leading off to the left? Where would that get him? It didn't seem to be the most logical place to hide. It didn't seem to lead to anywhere except to the front.

And maybe that was his purpose, she realized with a flash of insight.

Maybe he wasn't planning on running through this darkened corridor. Why would he do that after all, when he had a perfectly good vehicle parked out front?

It could be that he had gotten out of the back as the easiest exit, but that what he really planned to do was get away. And the way to do that would be in his car. By darting up this passage, and then getting away on the main road.

She and Connor reached the same conclusion at exactly the same time.

"He's going for the parking lot. He's going to drive out of here. That's what he's doing," Connor realized.

If Cami had thought he was running fast before, it was nothing compared to the speed he now showed as he turned up the alleyway, storming along the path to the building's front. Cami followed, her legs burning, her breath gasping in her throat, as she tried to keep up with Connor's long strides.

Their hunch was right, she realized. Ahead, a car door slammed.

And then they burst out into the warehouse's front yard, in time to see the blinding glare of headlights. An engine's roar split the night.

He was getting away! This was what he'd intended to do. Double back, grab his car, and flee the scene. For all she knew, he might be intending to go further. Flee the state. Hide out. Avoid them for long enough for this case to go cold.

"Stop!" Connor shouted, racing for the car. Cami's heart leaped into her mouth. What would it take to stop this man? Connor was putting himself in danger, at risk of being run down or hit by the car, that was for sure. With a flare of adrenaline, she realized how much risk he took on in his everyday work. A chase down meant balancing on a knife-edge of variables, and a perilous outcome was all too likely.

And what could she do? In this emergency situation, none of her hacking skills would help. The only other choice she had was to try and physically block the car, since it wasn't even electric.

The gate, she realized. The warehouse gate. At the moment, it was standing open, and if he got out of that gate, he would be gone. But if she could get there in time, she could close it.

Connor was racing for the car, and the shadows veered sharply as it backed at speed out of the bay.

Cami made a dash for the gate, giving it everything she had, not wasting a moment worrying about Connor now, but putting all her strength into grabbing the edge of the heavy steel gate and dragging it closed.

She heard an angry shout and a clatter of feet, and guessed that Connor had been forced to leap out of the way of the car, or be mown down.

And then, the headlights were blazing around in a sharp arc, and the car's engine reached a scream, and Cami felt her breath, hot and harsh in her throat.

Her legs burned. The rust-flecked steel bit into her hands. It was painful, cutting into her palm, and she didn't know if she'd be strong enough to get that heavy gate, on its protesting hinges, where she needed it to be in time. This could all go so horribly wrong, and now she was pinned by high-beam headlights, blinding and terrifying, as he aimed the car at the gate in what was now a race against time.

For a moment, she felt a chill of pure dread that she was going to be too slow, that he'd sideswipe the gate and her, that he'd burst through and be gone while she sprawled onto the blacktop, bleeding and hurt with broken bones.

And then, with a final gasping effort, she dragged the gate closed.

Brakes screeched, and smoke billowed from the tires as Nolan braked to an emergency stop with the hood just inches from the gate. With a pounding of feet, Connor was at the car door, wrenching it open, grabbing Nolan by his dark jacket and pulling him out.

"You're under arrest," he gasped. "Failure to comply, fleeing and eluding, and reckless endangerment. There may be more once we’ve questioned you. And you'd better be ready to give us answers."

CHAPTER SEVENTEEN

It gave Cami an uneasy chill to see Nolan sitting in the FBI interview room, pinned on the hard chair, under the bright, unrelenting overhead light. It brought back her own experience, just a couple of weeks earlier when she'd been on that side of a similar desk in the same building herself.

And she could be there again. The knowledge simmered uneasily within her. Who had traced her hurried exit from the archives, following that breadcrumb trail of her sister's corrupted case file?

Trouble lurked ahead, and the fact it hadn't yet hit her hard, didn't mean it wasn't going to. In fact it was worse, because trouble might be biding its time.

Connor opened the door and led the way into the room, bringing Cami's mind back to their current situation. What was important now was solving this crime, and in this chair, they had a strong suspect.

Nolan stared at them. His pale, dramatic stage make-up was smudged, and his dark hair, which had been gelled back for the movie role, was now flopping untidily over his face.

And yet he didn't seem to want to be cooperative. His arrogant expression had not budged while he was being processed, and his crossed arms were a clear indication of his contrary mindset.

Connor didn't seem in the least perturbed by this early show of resistance. Cami guessed he was just glad to have this man in the FBI offices, and not at large in the back streets of the warehouse district.

"Mr. Nolan," he said firmly, sitting in a chair opposite and checking the recording equipment. The action of double-checking seemed to be automatic, Cami saw, something he did without even thinking. "You know why you're here?"

Nolan pressed his thin lips together and shrugged. Then, reluctantly, he spoke, "You broke into our filming session. You entered without permission. And you're asking why I'm here?"

"The door was opened to us," Connor said calmly, countering this accusation with the ease of long expertise.

"I still don't understand what the hell you were doing there," Nolan insisted. "You gave us all a huge fright. I literally thought this was an armed robbery in progress. You know, we are at risk when we film late. Robberies often happen."

"You don't know what we were doing there? Let me explain. We're investigating a series of murders."

"And you've brought me in? How am I connected with all of this?"

"The victims' names are Brooke Perkins and Cleo Booth. Do you know those names?"

Cami knew this was an important question, even a pivotal one. But to her disappointment, he kept his face entirely blank.

He was an actor, she reminded herself. He didn't only produce movies but starred in them too. And an actor might be able to suppress the natural flare of guilt that hearing those names would produce. Especially if he was cunning, thinking ahead, and had expected to hear them.

"You've got a fake social media account in the name of Peter Frost," Connor said.

Again, Cami had hoped for more reaction, but Nolan nodded calmly. "I have a few different accounts."

"Why's that?"

"I'm a filmmaker. I'm a studier of human psychology. It's helpful to me in my work."

"You made threats to both the victims before they died."

Nolan shrugged. "Some of the films I make are edgy. They push people's buttons. I like to know how that plays out in real life. What the reactions are in groups, when threats are made. Who says what. Assuming you equate social media to real life."

The supercilious expression was, if anything, more obvious now, and Cami found herself briefly hating him for it.

Connor was, on the other hand, far more in control. He seemed resigned to the fact that he wasn't going to get a full confession out of Nolan any time soon. But he kept on questioning him. Pressing him.

"Threats made to both victims, just a few days before they both died? That seems like a huge coincidence."

"Strange, but true, I guess."

“Made under a fake profile?”

“I explained that already.”

Cami watched Nolan's expression for any sign of shock or dismay. Until now, there had been nothing that seemed to push him out of his totally unconcerned facade. But looking more closely at him, she sensed that he was starting to be uncomfortable with this line of questioning. She wasn't an expert in picking up these signals, but he was beginning to fidget. His long, bony fingers were rubbing together, and a shuffling noise under the desk told her he was tapping one foot against the other.

"It's a big coincidence, and I'd like to discuss it some more. You need to tell us how you knew these two victims, and why you made the threats you did," Connor said, clearly also picking up that they might be pushing Nolan to a place where he was ready to talk.

"I don't believe what I wrote online can possibly incriminate me."

A sudden thought occurred to Cami.

He'd said 'other profiles'. That meant he had more than one. They had only found Peter Frost so far, and on seeing those threats, they had stopped there. But what if there were other fake profiles associated with this strange, arrogant man, and he'd made more serious threats using them? Maybe that's why he was starting to look uncomfortable, she reasoned.

Tuning out Connor's relentless questioning, Cami opened her phone, discreetly glanced down, and went looking for further links. She knew she'd have to work quickly and that in the time, she might not be able to pick up what she needed. But if she was able to, then this might get them the breakthrough they needed. Because at the moment, Nolan seemed smug in the knowledge that he knew something they didn't—yet.

And then, with a widening of her eyes, she found it. There were two linked profiles. And one of them, Nash Taylor, hadn't stopped with making overt threats. Nash Taylor had sent messages. Cami read them, feeling quite horrified. These messages were nasty. They were most definitely threatening.

He'd messaged Brooke a week ago.

"You'd better be careful what you say online. Because you never know who might be waiting in real life. Got a good lock on your door?"

Cami gritted her teeth. This could get them somewhere, she was sure of it.

She waited for a pause in the questioning and then, in a casual voice, she said, "Tell us about Nash Taylor, Nolan, why don't you?"

She'd done it, she saw, feeling a thrill of satisfaction at the shock that was now evident on his face. Connor's quick, surprised glance was the only sign he gave of this bombshell.

"Nash Taylor seems to have specialized in messaging people privately. That's not conducting experiments in groups. That's one on one. It's serious. I think those messages would be dynamite if they were read out to a jury, especially the one you sent to Brooke last week."

In a slow, clear voice, Cami read it out again. It sounded even worse when spoken.

There was a long, drawn-out silence. The man sitting opposite them obviously wasn't used to being cornered. He had probably survived on the strength of his bluffing skills in tough situations for years, but now he had nowhere to go. No room to maneuver. His gaze was darting everywhere and she was sure that now, he felt utterly trapped.

"I don't know anything about Nash Taylor," Nolan spat back, his bravado suddenly deserting him.

"How can you say that?" Connor said, sounding almost amused by this change in the suspect's mindset. "It's one of your alternative profiles."

"No, it isn't!" Now he looked panicked.

"It's very clearly linked to your profile. I can show you the step-by-step process I used to confirm that," Cami said. “I think a jury would be able to follow it quite easily.”

Nolan let out a long, shaky breath.

"Look, I'll be truthful with you, okay? I promise. I don't want to get into trouble for this. I . . . I didn't think you would find that profile. It changes often because it gets blocked and removed. But I . . . I had it for a reason."

"And what reason is that?" Connor said.

"Justice." The word sounded weak and unconvincing on Nolan's lips. "I know it's wrong, but I hate seeing the bullying that goes on in the online world. The way people hide behind their anonymity and taunt and torment others. I can't handle it. And I used that profile when I wanted to make sure that someone listened—really listened—when I thought they had behaved in a way that was out of line."

"And did you take that further? Decide to mete out this justice in real life?"

"No!" Nolan twined his finger together anxiously. "No, I would not do that. But I knew how it would look if you did find those profiles and saw that I'd made the threats. I didn't want to get in trouble for . . . for trying to make things right in the world."

Connor looked at him for a long moment.

"Can you account for your movements earlier this morning at approximately seven a.m.?"

Nolan thought for a moment. Then, with a defeated sigh, he looked down. "I can't. I was home alone. I was asleep."

"And two days ago, in the evening?"

Nolan now looked hunted. "Every weekday until tonight, I've been working late. Editing, splicing."

"Alone?"

"Yes, alone!" Nolan shot back. Now, Cami saw, this tall, strongly built man was starting to sweat.

“Did you ever meet either of the victims in real life?”

“I—look, I don’t know. I’d be lying if I said no. I do a lot of work in communal areas, cafés, artists’ retreats. I find those environments inspiring. I see a lot of people there. It could be that I bumped into them. I don’t want to say no, and then you show me camera footage of me saying hi to one of them? Know what I mean? I accept I might have seen or spoken to them, but I didn’t seek them out.”

"The knife you used on set. It looked like a serious weapon."

"It's part of a set. A chef's knife."

"Sharp?"

"Yes, of course it's sharp."

"What did you do with it?"

"I . . . I threw it away. As I ran." He blinked rapidly.

“And you’re left handed.”

“I am. So what? A lot of creative people are!”

They had a panicking suspect who had made overt threats and who was open about his desire for revenge on cyber bullies. He'd had a knife in his possession when they arrived, that he'd since disposed of.

Cami was starting to think that this case was ready to wrap up, and that they were looking at the killer. A man who was breaking more badly with every moment that passed.

Then, there was a knock on the interview room door.

Not wanting to interrupt Connor's flow, Cami jumped up and went to the door. She quickly stepped outside.

Her eyes widened in surprise as she came face to face with Ethan.

"Hey there," she whispered, smiling at this unexpected sight.

“Hey, Cami. It’s good to see you.”

Although Ethan’s words were warming, she realized the tall, brown-haired, cute agent wasn't returning her smile. In fact, he looked highly stressed.

"You need to get Connor out here. Straight away," he whispered back. "There's just been another murder called in, and it's the same MO. Same message left. This time, he's killed a woman in Southdale."

CHAPTER EIGHTEEN

Cami felt utterly horrified by this bombshell as she stared at Ethan.

"Just been called in?" she asked. "Like, how long ago?"

"Recently. Time of death, maybe an hour or two ago," Ethan said, and her heart plummeted.

An hour or two ago, Nolan had been filming. There was no way he could have been in Southdale committing these crimes. Southdale was too far from the warehouse area. His protests, though flimsy-sounding, had been valid. He wasn't the killer.

The killer was still at large, and had struck again.

"I'll go get him," Cami said. She went back into the interview room and tapped Connor on the shoulder.

"Urgent," she mouthed.

He stood up and hustled outside.

"Don't tell me there's been another one," he said to Ethan, as soon as the interview room door was closed.

Ethan nodded, his brow furrowed with tension. "An hour or two ago. Southdale. Same MO."

Connor shook his head.

"We'd better get to the scene. Hold this suspect here for now, until we can confirm the timing. Come on," he said to Cami, already turning to stride down the corridor.

As she followed, Cami realized her mind was hazy with exhaustion. It was after eleven p.m. now. This case was intense and seemed unrelenting. And now, there was a fresh murder scene?

Connor climbed in the car and got on the radio.

"We're on our way to Southdale," he said tersely. "Bring me up to speed. What happened?"

"A woman called Emma Pratley was killed. Same message left online. It popped up about an hour and a half ago on a public forum. Someone put two and two together, called the police, and they went to her home and found her."

"Hopefully there's some evidence at the scene," Connor muttered, accelerating as he reached the main road.

Surely there was a chance of it, she hoped. Given that he was speeding up his rate of killings, and that this was the second one today.

While Connor raced to the scene, Cami knew there wasn't time to stew in her shock. She needed to forget about her tiredness and add value to their team. To start, she began looking up background on Emma Pratley. It would help to know who she was, Cami reasoned.

"She's a blogger and influencer. She works in the fashion world," Cami told Connor.

"Any evidence of cyberbullying? That seems to be our main common thread. Look for it," he said.

"I'll need to find out where she interacts. I can see already that she has strong opinions," Cami said.

Emma was thirty-four years old, she saw, making her the oldest victim so far, and she had previously worked as a model before turning her hand to fashion blogging. Cami guessed that had been the next logical step in her career. She was a beautiful woman, with thick brunette hair, strong bone structure, and a look in her sea green eyes that told Cami she didn't suffer fools easily.

"Yes, she has been active online. And I have seen some nasty comments," Cami said, with a twist of her stomach, as she dug deeper.

She'd found the place where the words had been written.

Just an hour ago, on a local style and fashion group, those all-caps words had been left on her profile.

It had attracted some anxious comments from a few others, prompting the call to the police. There had even been some debate about whether this comment should be removed.

"Everything okay?"

"Why did you write that, Emma?"

"Emma, did you write it? Guys, is this not what happened in those other murders? I heard something this afternoon."

"ADMIN REMOVE THE COMMENT NOW IT'S DISGUSTING!"

"No! Admin, leave the comment. It might be evidence. Does anyone know where she lives? Someone should check up on her!"

But in spite of this concerned flurry, many others had simply ignored it, and Cami guessed they were just glad she'd stopped commenting and had no idea of what had played out. Most likely, they weren't aware of what those words meant. The case had not yet made national headlines, although she had seen it start to dominate on the local news. She guessed that the FBI was keeping the details under wraps so as not to cause panic or alert the suspect that they were on his trail.

Finally, Connor pulled up outside a small suburban home, set well back from the road. There was a police cruiser parked outside along with a couple of unmarked cars and emergency response vehicles, and the place was swarming with cops.

Glancing to the side of the house, Cami saw the neighbors were watching anxiously, and a few other locals had congregated, looking as if they'd climbed hastily out of bed, rumple-haired, pale-faced, and stressed looking.

She couldn't believe this had happened so fast. Was the speed causing him to make errors? As they approached the neat, well-maintained home, Cami looked around for any cameras and was disappointed to see none.

"Evening, gents," Connor greeted the nearest cops with professional familiarity.

"The victim is in the lounge," the cop said. "Nasty scene. I hope we can catch this guy soon or we're going to have major panic on our hands."

Nasty scene? Cami felt sick with anticipation of what she might find there.

“Any evidence? Any camera footage?” Connor asked.

“Nothing so far. We’ve sent a patrol out on foot to look for any cameras, but there are none on this street,” the cop said regretfully.

She saw Connor give an assessing glance at the front door, whose latch was twisted and had clearly been forced. So this was how the killer had gotten in, bold and brutal.

Connor and Cami walked inside, both of them pulling on gloves and snapping on foot covers over their shoes.

They entered the house, stepping through from the small hallway into the lounge.

It was a warm, attractive room. There was a large comfy sofa, a love seat, and a well-stocked bookshelf beneath a flatscreen TV.

And Cami drew in a shocked breath as she saw the victim, tall and slender, collapsed face down on the floor near the archway that led to the kitchen. Her hands were outstretched, as if reaching for someone to save her. There was a dark stain on the back of her royal blue top. Her long hair, fanned around her, was flecked with blood.

For a moment, Cami felt the room spin sickeningly, and she quickly looked away, breathing deep. She knew this was a bad one, and she really didn't need all the gory details in front of her to cement the gruesome sight in her mind.

Instead, she looked around the room, averting her eyes from the scene.

Emma's laptop was still open on the coffee table. This was where he'd typed the words. Her purse was on the floor. Perhaps her phone was in there. There was an empty wineglass and a half-full mug of coffee on the table.

She'd been working late, but she hadn't just been doing work. She'd been fighting online, and it had gotten her killed. Those final, awful, all-caps words had come at the end of an argument.

At any rate, the argument had ended once they'd been typed, she thought, shivering.

"There's her phone," Cami said, seeing a bright cover peeking out of her purse.

"We'll take that in evidence," Connor said. "When you've finished wrapping up the scene, bag it for us, please?" he asked one of the cops.

Taking a final look around, he turned away.

"Let's go see if any of the neighbors heard or saw anything," he said.

He headed outside and made his way purposefully over to the knot of people standing there.

"Evening," he said briskly. "I'm sorry this has happened. I know how shocked you must be feeling now."

There were somber nods all around as they took in his sympathetic words. Connor continued. "This case is a top priority for us. Any information might be helpful. Did any of you hear or see anything?"

Cami was expecting a whole series of nos, but to her surprise one of the women standing nearby nodded.

"Yes. I heard a car racing away about an hour ago. I was wondering who it was, because we usually don't hear sounds like that nearby here. But it seemed to come from down the road." She pointed.

"Any idea on the sound? Sports car, sedan, larger vehicle?"

"I would say a powerful car. But I don't know enough to be sure. I wish I'd looked out and seen it," she said regretfully.

"Thanks, that's helpful all the same," Connor said.

Cami guessed that either the killer had parked farther down, or else the neighbor had only picked up the sound when he'd passed. At any rate, it showed to her again that this man moved quickly. He researched his targets, he knew their homes, he could find them unerringly, and he got in and out at a time when he knew they would be alone, and it was safe for him. He even chose the places he stopped with some care.

How was he locating them? Why these victims? There were thousands of cyberbullies in Boston. What made him choose these ones?

Connor wrapped up his questioning of the neighbors and turned to trudge back toward the scene.

“Can you access that phone now?” he asked.

Cami made a face. “It’s a very new iPhone, and I might be able to hack it, but it will take a few hours. Those phones aren’t a quick fix.”

"Then we’ll have another look around, see if there’s any more evidence, and if there isn’t, we’ll turn in. There’s not much more we can do tonight. We'll start again first thing tomorrow morning," he muttered to Cami.

Suddenly, an idea occurred to Cami as she trailed behind Connor, feeling tired, discouraged, and frustrated.

It was an idea that had come from the seed that Nolan had planted. He’d said he spent a lot of time in communal areas and cafés where trendy people congregated. Since all the victims so far were active online and had associated jobs, perhaps this was how they’d been hunted.

Maybe this killer was using a certain location as his starting point. For one, that would make sure he was only targeting locals. And if he was in their close proximity, getting other information might be easier too. So maybe, rather than searching for a person, they should search for a place.

As the cop at the door completed the initial paperwork and handed Connor the plastic evidence bag he'd requested, Cami felt her hopes lift again. With two of the victims' phones in their possession, she could see if her theory might pan out.

CHAPTER NINETEEN

Cami paced around her motel room, her mind racing, wishing that she could fast-forward time to tomorrow, so that she could see if it was possible to log into Emma's phone. That might provide clearer answers. It was stomach-churning to think that this killer was still ahead of them, still plotting, perhaps even stalking his next victim.

Three kills. Three kills they had been unable to prevent. She didn't even want to think about that hushed murder scene, those knots of apprehensive, traumatized people outside, that woman sprawled on the floor.

How was she going to sleep? It felt like an impossibility.

Connor had checked them into a basic, downtown place, and had bought them each a burger and a bottle of water. Her basic toiletries, toothbrush, and a spare shirt and underwear stowed in her laptop bag were all she needed for an overnight stay.

This time, Connor hadn't booked the adjoining room, but had checked into one on the other side of the forecourt. Cami guessed that might mean he trusted her more now. At any rate, he seemed to have faith that she wouldn't do a midnight run and escape.

Feeling suddenly like some friendly company, she decided to give into temptation and text Ethan. Maybe he was still up.

"Hey. You there?" she texted.

"Hey, Cami! Yes. Here. How's today been for you?"

"It's been tough. Tell me, do you ever get used to dealing with murder?"

"Nope. It stays tough for me. I deal with it mostly by watching lots of bad comedy movies and doing gym workouts."

Cami found herself smiling. Ethan was funny.

"I think that sounds like a good idea. Neither possible right now, but both on the list for later."

"Your name's been mentioned a lot since you were last here."

"It has? How?"

"Connor said you are the most rebellious partner he ever had to work with, but he's seriously impressed by your IT skill, and how fast

you pick things up. He's worked with other experts before. As have I. We both agree you're better."

Cami felt relieved by that. "*Glad to know it. He doesn't give much away."*

"Connor keeps his defenses up very high at work. But under them, he's a softie," Ethan shared.

"Who are the flowers from? There were flowers in his office?"

"They are from his girlfriend. She's waiting to see if he's going to be deployed here on a more permanent basis. If so, she's moving here to be with him. So he told me. She does projects all over the country, so she's mobile, and apparently, they're really missing each other!"

"Oh, that's very cute," Cami texted. Clearly, Connor did have hidden romantic depths. She was now wondering if Ethan had a girlfriend.

"What about you? Anyone special in your life?"

There was a pause. At that moment, before Ethan had replied, her phone began ringing loudly.

Was this Connor? Surely there couldn't have been another murder? With her heart in her throat at the thought, Cami rushed over to pick up the call, noticing that it was from the FBI office number.

Immediately, her thoughts rushed to Fraser. He'd hinted that there was trouble ahead. Was it going to land on her now?

Quickly, she picked up the call. Better to get it over with.

"Hello, Cami speaking," she said.

A rich, confident woman's voice resonated down the line. A familiar voice to Cami.

"Ms. Lark. It's Jacenta here."

"Oh. Hi. I mean, good evening," Cami said.

The vision of the tall, imposing, dark-eyed woman came into her mind. Jacenta was her probation officer. Cami hadn't even known she was going to be assigned such a person, but apparently, after you'd committed a crime against the FBI and they took you on to help with a case, you earned yourself one.

Cami thought that Jacenta had instinctively disapproved of her. She'd gotten that strong impression when they'd met on her first case. She knew she'd have to work hard to earn this scary agent's trust and approval.

"I hear you're back on a case," Jacenta said, getting straight to the point.

"Yes. I was called in again."

"Fraser informed me of that. He said you're contracted for a year, to help on cases where you can add value."

Cami couldn't decide, from her tone, if Jacenta thought that was a good or bad thing.

"Yes," she said simply, unsure what else to say.

"For as long as you're on duty with the organization, I'll be touching base with you."

"Thank you," Cami said humbly.

"Any problems, any issues?"

"No, not really. Today was difficult."

"In what way?"

"We didn't make progress. I felt like I couldn't do enough on the case. And also, I . . . I battle with looking at dead bodies. We had to see two different ones today. Well, two locations. Three bodies. At the pathologist's office, and at a crime scene." She paused. "Does it ever get easier?"

"It's never easy. But it does get less traumatic. You learn how to compartmentalize. You just have to tell yourself that what you're doing is right. That it's a necessary part of fighting crime. To me, viewing the scene and the bodies is a sign of respect. We're respecting that even in death, they tried to tell us something, and we need to listen."

Cami thought that was a very interesting perspective, as Jacenta continued. "And you're doing alright with Connor this time? No conflicts?"

"Not really," Cami admitted, shifting the phone to her other hand. "I'm getting better at working with him as I go along. I think I am. I hope, anyway."

"Well, keep me informed if anything changes. I want to know about any hiccups anywhere. Any problems with this investigation, with Connor—anything at all."

"Will do. I promise. Thank you."

"And get some sleep," Jacenta said sternly. "Especially if you've had a tough day, you might feel as if you're too stressed to rest. But remember, if you're exhausted, you won't work well tomorrow. Force yourself to relax. Don't allow yourself to dwell on what happened today. Take your thoughts to a happy place, you hear?"

Surprised, Cami found herself grinning at that.

"I will," she said.

Jacenta cut the call, and taking her advice, Cami stopped pacing and got into bed.

There, she finally read Ethan’s message.

“I don’t have a girlfriend. It’s just the bad movies and gym workouts for now. But maybe I need to change that sometime?”

Cami felt her stomach flip. That definitely sounded flirtatious.

“Maybe you do!” she texted back. Then, smiling, she plugged her phone in to charge and turned over. She felt better now, and the horrors of the day had receded.

Tomorrow, she would wake with a fresh mind and be ready to carry on the chase. Tomorrow, she promised herself, she would do whatever it took to find this killer.

***

Cami’s theory hinged on whether she could access the second phone. And as she jolted upright from a surprisingly deep sleep in the motel room, she saw that it was now six a.m. and that meant it was time to check.

Ideally, she needed three phones. But with two, she could make a plan.

The program she'd set to run to open Emma’s phone would have been hard at work, and she hoped by now she might have access. The password system on that very new phone was complex and hard to bypass.

She got dressed, moving around the neat, impersonal motel room with its blue-gray décor and framed prints of Boston architecture and then walked across the forecourt to Connor's room and tapped on the door.

Connor opened the door just a moment later. He was dressed, and looked as if he'd been awake for some time already.

"Come on in," he said. "Let's see if you can open it. And now, run this theory past me again? What are we looking for? Remember that these phones have been temporarily released to us so that we can work on their content, but they still need to be signed back into evidence, so for now, wear gloves when you handle them."

Heading over to the desk where the phones lay, attached to chargers, Cami told him again about the idea that had fleetingly come to her last night.

"It started out with me thinking that we haven't focused enough on why the killer has chosen these particular victims," she said, pulling on the gloves Connor had placed nearby.

"Because they're bullies?"

"But why them? There must some method he's using to find them initially. A reason why they're on the shortlist. And a reason why he's been able to find three bullies who all live in Boston."

"Yeah. I guess people can troll online from anywhere," Connor conceded.

"I think he might have a real life location where he's picking them. Like a hunting ground, where he finds his prey and then he targets them. Perhaps he does that by using a common wi-fi network. And he could do that, because the second part of my theory, is that we haven't yet figured out how tech savvy this guy is. And he is tech savvy. He's been able to get a lot of details on his victims."

"Yes. Those scenes are clean. And his speed points to thorough research," Connor agreed.

"So what I was wondering was whether there might be somewhere they've all been working at some stage. Some communal café, artists' center, or hub. They all live within about a ten mile radius, and they could all have used the same place at some point."

"And that would have helped the killer how?" Connor said.

As she took the phone off the charger, Cami explained in more detail.

"If the café had an open IP address, and a shared network, he could have gotten a lot of details from them online. Open wi-fi and shared networks are a hacker's best friend, and especially if people are just messing around on social media or doing basic work, they often don't care."

"Yup, I can see that," Connor said.

"He could have logged in, seen who they were, what they were saying, and he might even have been able to find out where they lived. Assuming he has a good knowledge of tech."

"And can you find out if there was a place in common?" Connor asked.

It was the million-dollar question, but as Cami took a look at the phone, she realized that she had the first step, at least.

"I've got into Emma's phone, so now I have two devices to check. So, what I'm going to do now, is try and see where those victims have been."

"And you're going to do that how?" Connor asked.

"I'm going to look at their saved locations, their check-ins, their payments, their messages. I'll check their saved wi-fi records."

“And all that’s available?”

“Well, sort of. Some of it isn't obvious and some of it is hidden, but it's a lot easier if you have their personal devices. Then you can pretty much retrace their steps."

Connor shook his head. "It doesn't make total sense to me, but if you can get in and find these details, then let's see," he said in tones of reluctant approval.

Cami felt a mixture of satisfaction and relief at Connor's grudging praise. If she could put all of the victims' details together, that might give them something to work with. And she was looking, particularly, for places where they would have used the wi-fi. Where there would have been a chance for someone to see who they were, what they were doing, and what they were saying.

"Where's Cleo's phone?" Cami said, thinking again of how useful a third device would be.

"Cleo's phone was damaged. It seemed like she was also about to call for help when he broke in. She dropped it and then fell on it when she died. The screen smashed," Connor said.

"Okay. I'll see what I can do without the phone. I may be able to get something else online or from her social media," Cami said.

She was aware of Connor drawing back the curtains to let in the gray light of early dawn, and from somewhere in this urban environment, she picked up a hint of birdsong. But her focus was on the interactions. On patiently tracing where these victims had been in the weeks before their death. Brooke had been out and about nonstop. Cami guessed that she might have been meeting with clients and then working nearby. So perhaps Emma, the most recent victim, would provide an easier set of movements to match with.

Cami focused on her check-ins, cross-referencing where Emma had been and then comparing those to the other two.

She thought she had a common thread for a brief, exciting moment, but then couldn't find anything to confirm it on Cleo's interactions. So she went back further, another week into the past, and then she saw something that looked like it could be a match.

"Here. I've got something. I can't see where it's originating from yet. But all of them, in their browsing history, have connected up with this same wi-fi router," Cami said.

"A router?"

"Emma used it frequently. Brooke used it a few times in the past month. And Cleo used it a couple of weeks ago, according to what I can see here."

"So where is it?"

"It'll be based somewhere accessible. Most likely in a public location."

"How do we find it?"

"I need to go and hunt for it," Cami said.

Focusing intently on her task, she began the search, using a program that would help her to align the IP addresses with the geographic locations. It was a time consuming task and the level of concentration required was all the way on the top end of the spectrum. Cami focused intently as she searched. She was narrowing it down and felt a thrill of anticipation as she identified the suburb. The location of this router was in a central location to where the victims lived. And it was on the outskirts of downtown Boston. That much, she knew, even though it still felt like fumbling in the dark as she struggled to narrow down the options. Where was it?

Seething with impatience, she ran the program again, coordinating it with the mapping software to try and get an answer. The secret lay in triangulating the signal strength, but finding the information on this was like stumbling through a long tunnel, looking for a hidden alcove.

With a sigh, Cami looked up.

To her surprise, she saw the windows were substantially brighter than they had been when she began her hunt. Daylight was streaming in. From outside, the faint birdsong had been replaced with the throb and thrum of traffic.

"You found it?" Connor sounded impatient.

"I've got it to within a few blocks," Cami said, feeling frustrated that she couldn't triangulate it more precisely from this hotel room. "But if we go to that area, I might be able to get closer."

Connor didn't answer, but headed purposefully toward the door.

CHAPTER TWENTY

Cami had her laptop and phone open as Connor drove slowly into the downtown block where this router was located—somewhere. She was working at top speed, juggling her devices as best she could on the car seat. She had a very strong feeling that this place was the venue they needed.

All the variables were racing through her mind. For sure, this had to be the common thread. All three had been there.

But where was it?

The area wasn't helping. It was a trendy, slightly seedy mishmash of restaurants, bars, cafés, and clubs. An ideal student haunt, with charming, tumbledown, picturesque locations at every turn and with a medley of different chairs, faded wall art, rickety tables, and tiny but well-stocked bars. There were probably fifty different places within this three-block radius where these journalists and bloggers might have worked. Narrowing them down was not going to be easy, especially since they were all in such close proximity, crammed together in the labyrinth of narrow, twisting streets.

It was going to be a process of trial and error to find this place.

"Turn left here," she said.

Nope. This wasn't getting her anywhere.

"Turn around," she said.

With a sigh that told Cami he was starting to think knocking on doors might just get them better answers, Connor obliged.

"Try this street?" she suggested. This was a tiny road that wound its way in between a cluttered, multi-level shopping area. A tourist would be busy all day exploring these nooks and crannies. Cami didn't have all day and was starting to feel despairing about getting closer.

Did one of these shops have an internet café in the back room, she wondered. It felt as if she was in the right place, but frustratingly, as Connor inched his way along the road, Cami wasn't getting what she needed. The signal wasn't improving and was remaining at the same level.

How was that possible, she wondered.

And then, she looked up.

"There! That must be it," she said.

Above the shops, she saw a surprisingly large and very atmospheric looking café.

"The Art House Café," it read in dark lettering above the door, which was accessed by a steep staircase.

"The Art House Café? What can I find about it? Can you stop for a moment?" Cami asked.

"Not without causing a traffic obstruction," Connor grumbled, but a minute later he found a place to pull over.

"Yup, this is their router. And it looks as if it's quite the trendy destination for online activities. There's a dark web browser on this main machine that I'm picking up." Cami frowned. "And linked to that, there's some videos on here, in the archives, that look weird."

"How do you mean?"

"I don't know. I'm not picking up enough to be sure."

"Pornographic?" Connor asked.

"Not pornographic." Cami was able to see more as her homemade hack got her further in. "But it looks as if he has some concealed cameras in the restaurant. There's some footage of a couple of the customers. Just coming in, going out. But they're all women. There are a few more here too. I'm wondering if he kept the footage when someone he liked walked in. Or maybe not someone he liked," she said thoughtfully.

"Any videos of the victims?" Connor pushed.

"I'm looking."

"And?" Connor's tone seethed with impatience as if Cami wasn't already working fast enough to set her keyboard on fire.

"I think there's some of Emma here. Yes, it's her for sure. He took a video of her walking in, and there's also footage of her heading for the restrooms." Cami felt creeped out by that. "She was filmed most recently, in the last few days. There are a lot of these short videos, and I mean a lot. If I go back, I might find the others."

"Go back," Connor said.

"Okay. I'm doing it. Hang on." There was firewall software on the attack here, seeking to infiltrate her defenses. Quickly, Cami exited and re-entered, this time with an additional layer of camouflage in place that she hoped would buy her more time.

"Yes. I've found Cleo," she said triumphantly. "And here's Brooke, I'm almost sure. But I need to get out again. I'm being chased."

As she hurriedly backtracked, Cami felt utterly shocked by these small snippets of recorded footage. How weird and creepy was it to film your customers going about their work and then save the videos? Or was there another reason for doing that? Was he hoping to zoom in on their screens later, taking information that he could use to find them?"

Suspicion crystallized in her mind.

This suspect was most definitely up to something strange, but how far had his forays into his clients' privacy gone?

"Who is this man?" she asked, feeling outraged. "Shall I look him up?"

"Why do you need to do that?" Connor said.

"To find out about him," Cami argued.

"There's no need for that." He indicated the windows above. "We can go right in and ask to speak to him."

While Cami was busy exploring the Art House Café online, the place had opened for the day. The blinds were up, the main door was flung wide, and beyond it, she could see a place that looked to be full of dark, trendy décor, with unique, edgy, and strategically lit paintings on the walls: vibrant animals in bright colors, upside-down neon landscapes, glittery spider webs, and futuristic scenes.

"Okay," she said. "Let's go up."

They managed to find a parking space after a frustrating five-minute drive around this crowded area. And then they climbed the stairs and walked through the door, into this surprisingly dark setup.

Bright screens glowed at intervals, with signage advertising that these were rental devices for people who didn't bring their own. Everything about that setup screamed "you'll be hacked" to Cami.

Already, as they were looking for parking, the first few customers had filtered in. They were sitting on the medley of available chairs, sofas, armchairs, bean bags, and Pilates balls that surrounded the tables. There were plugs and adapters literally everywhere. The air smelled of good coffee with a faint undertone of toasted bread.

Even though Cami felt deeply suspicious of this place, she also felt drawn to the environment. She couldn't help it. The blinding speed of the connectivity—advertised on a handwritten poster by the door. The smell of coffee. The variety of quirky seats. The darkness of the décor, and the uniqueness of the art pieces on the walls. It was trendy, and it was fun. She would have loved to work here, with the most stringent security in place, of course.

Now she could see why Emma had regarded this place as a favorite local haunt, and why Cleo and Brooke, both clearly fans of the ultimate environment, had spent time here.

But now, the owner had some answers to give, and Connor was already striding over to the reception console nestled into the wall, with bright colored lights above it.

"We need to speak to the guy in charge here. Who's he?" he asked the young waitress, in a black apron, who appeared on the other side of the console.

She stared at him dubiously. "He's Hayden Mars. Who are you?" she asked, in a world-weary tone.

Connor didn't show any signs of being put off by her attitude.

"FBI Special Agent Connor," he said, showing his badge. Cami guessed it was not a familiar sight in this safe, secluded haunt.

"Uh—he's not here," she stammered.

"Where is he?" Connor demanded.

"I don't know."

Now she sounded close to panic. Cami had the feeling that faced with trouble from the FBI or trouble from her boss, she was going to protect her boss and carry on claiming ignorance. After all, the FBI didn’t pay her salary, and jobs in a trendy place like this didn't come along every day.

But Cami was thinking again of those windows outside this café, and what she was seeing inside. It seemed to her that the inside was smaller than she had expected. She'd thought when they had climbed the stairs, that they would be in the center of the café. But in fact, the door was all the way on the left.

And that meant something else was on the far side. Walled off and invisible. It wasn't a kitchen. She saw a waitress with a tray emerge from the far right.

Suddenly, she wondered if the space on the far left might be an apartment. A guy like this, with this vision and these quirks, might have set up a combo working and living space.

"You are committing a federal crime if you refuse to disclose information," Connor was saying in a reasonable tone to the appalled looking waitress. Guessing that this conversation might take a while and would most likely end nowhere, Cami decided to take a look at the cameras.

That was easy enough. Although the internet itself was well protected here, as usual, nobody had bothered to secure the cameras.

She found their online presence immediately and, using the conveniently accessible wi-fi, logged in.

Here was the top camera, right above them, filming them as they stood. There were a few others dotted around the place. Two in the kitchen. One directed at the till.

And here was another one. What was this one?

Cami switched to its vantage point and her eyes narrowed.

This was an apartment. She was absolutely sure that it was the place to the left of where they were standing. The lighting was the same, the light from the windows looked identical. The shape of the windows was identical. Now, she could see an interleading door to the far left where it must be accessed from.

She saw a dimly lit lounge through the camera view, and she could also see, on a wall inside the apartment, a security camera screen that showed all the footage. Each one of the different camera vantage points was there, divided into eight neat sections, faraway but still discernible. Even from within his apartment, Hayden Mars could keep an eye on his business.

And then, as she watched the camera footage, a man with dark, lanky hair tied back in a ponytail strolled into the picture, staring down at the screen. A leather jacket gleamed on his shoulders. He switched on a lamp, and she saw the apartment was decorated darkly, in rich reds and blacks.

This was Hayden Mars. She was sure of it. He was holed up in his apartment, watching them on the screen. He wasn't coming out. But he didn't know they were watching him too.

She pulled him aside so the waitress couldn't hear.

"He's there!" Whispering, she pointed to him on her screen, and heard Connor's shocked intake of breath at the sight.

"He's hiding away in there," the agent said thoughtfully, and Cami knew he was grappling with solutions to this problem. They didn't yet have sufficient cause to enter the clearly locked premises where he was hiding, thinking he was safe and unobserved. But they had to get face to face with this suspect fast.

Would it be possible to flush him out, Cami wondered. Perhaps it could be done somehow—but how, Cami agonized. With the technology she'd been able to take over, what would work the best? She needed something that would provide shock value. That would scare him, and that would threaten him enough to flush him out.

“What are you thinking?” Connor whispered to her, sounding impatient.

“I was thinking of what we could do that might get him out. I think there could be a way,” she whispered.

Connor looked startled. “What exactly will be possible?” he asked, and she could clearly hear in his tone that at this point, he thought her capable of anything but was cautiously willing to see where this led.

“I can take over the speaker system. There’s an intercom system here that’s linked to the same app running the cameras. I think that’ll mean we can communicate with him in there. And it might just scare him out.”

“If a voice sounds from nowhere over the speaker, saying ‘I can see you in there?’” Connor suggested thoughtfully. Cami could see he was interested in her idea. That he thought it had potential.

"Exactly,” she said.

“Alright.” Connor paused for a while, as if gathering his thoughts. “Show me when it’s ready.”

“When I hold my finger down and you can see the red light, he'll hear you."

Cami couldn’t wait to see what Connor was going to come up with. This was going to be interesting, for sure. She hoped it would have the desired effect. At least they’d be able to see his reaction on the cameras.

She pressed her finger down to activate the control, and the red light started flashing.

CHAPTER TWENTY ONE

"Hayden Mars," Connor's voice boomed.

Cami had guessed that the microphone system was connected up to the entire café complex, not just to his apartment area. And it most definitely did have the anticipated shock value. The waiters looked around, startled, and on the camera feed, Cami saw Hayden jump visibly, staring in the direction of the door with something close to panic in his eyes.

"Hayden Mars, FBI here. We need you to come out of your apartment adjoining this café and speak to us. We can see you in there. We need to question you regarding a criminal investigation that involves your business."

Connor paused.

Looking around, Cami could see that this had caused a serious commotion. Clearly not wanting any of the clientele to hear anything more, the waitress was now rushing around, whispering to the scattering of customers and ushering them quickly outside. It looked as if, for now, she was closing the place up as Connor's threatening tones continued.

"We will interview you via your loudspeaker system if you remain in there. Or else, you can come out and speak with more privacy face to face." He paused. "You should probably know that we have a very skilled IT expert on our team. It seems your café is being closed now. Your customers are being asked to leave. That's not good for business. It'll stay closed for as long as you stay in there."

The silence that followed was resounding. Cami wished she could see Hayden's face on the cameras, but he'd turned away. His body language, however, was all about anxiety. His shoulders were hunched. His head was moving from side to side as if looking for a nonexistent solution to this crisis.

"I'll tell you what we're going to do first before we start asking questions," Connor said, clearly looking for hot buttons to press before he led up to the big whammy. "First, we're going to run all your licensing and permissions through our system to make sure it's all up to date. Then we're going to take a look at the building's structure to make sure it's one hundred percent legally compliant."

That was a good threat, Cami thought. In this old, historic-feeling warren of buildings, there was bound to be something that was not compliant or up to date.

But there was only silence from Hayden, who obviously thought this was a bluff, and they wouldn't find anything.

Connor then continued, sounding more triumphant now.

"We're then going to take a look at the camera setup within this establishment. We will access some of the footage you have stored online. We're going to make sure nothing's getting filmed illegally or stored illegally."

There was a moment of frozen silence, and Cami knew this threat had hit home.

Hayden turned to face the cameras and spread his arms in a gesture of defeat.

"I'll be out now," he said in a shaking voice.

They had their suspect. Triumphant as she felt, Cami kept watch on the cameras while the short time passed. She didn't want him sneaking out of any side doors and disappearing into the maze of streets. But it seemed that the threats had gotten the necessary results, because a minute and a half later, the interleading door banged open and Hayden marched out.

He looked the type to have a whole lot of underhanded activities on the go, Cami thought, wondering what she would have found if she'd kept searching a little longer. His eyes were shifty, and he couldn't keep eye contact with Connor for any length of time. But his height and build were right for the killer's.

"What was that all about?" he said, sounding short of breath. "Literally, you're harassing me."

"We need to talk," Connor said shortly. "Where can we do it?"

Hayden flinched, as if these words sounded like a threat. Then, he indicated the furthermost corner of the restaurant.

"We can talk there."

They headed to the four-seater table, which was near a vividly colored modern art painting that seemed to be of a tangle of wires.

Cami had no idea what the painting meant, but she hoped that getting the truth from their suspect wouldn't be as complex.

"What's this about?" he asked again as they sat down. "I don't see any reason for this. It's like you're trying to make me a scapegoat. What have I ever done?" His voice was shaking. Cami didn't trust the expression of innocence on his face at all. It looked as if it didn't belong there.

"We're here in connection with three recent murders."

"Why me? I'm no killer."

"All three victims were online, in your café, before their death."

"Look, is this about the two women who were stabbed? And those social media messages? I heard about those of course. I mean, it's big talk in the online circles right now."

"Three victims," Connor stated, eyeing him closely.

"I don't know anything about a third woman, and I had nothing to do with it. I'm just a venue. Because we're trendy and different, we get a lot of people working here. A lot of journos, bloggers, influencers. It would be a surprise if they hadn't been here."

Cami couldn't work out if he was telling the truth when he said he didn't know about the third murder. Was he faking it to try and prove his innocence? Or was his ignorance genuine? He was smart enough to do a clever fake, for sure. This was not a stupid man. There was cunning in his eyes.

"You run an internet café where you keep video footage of the customers. Female customers. Including the three victims. You keep the camera shots of them entering, leaving, heading to the restrooms. What's that about?"

Now, Hayden looked furtive as if this was a point of attack he couldn't easily counter.

"How do you know about that?" he asked defensively.

"We took a look around when we were tracing your router," Cami said and saw his eyes flicker her way. "Just to get some background information. We didn't expect to find so much of it."

Hayden looked briefly appalled that anyone had managed to access that footage.

"I was getting material for one of my channels," Hayden said, sounding forlorn. "I don't understand how that links me to their deaths."

"What do you mean?" Connor asked.

"Channels? I guess any café, any business, would have their own channel. I make YouTube videos, vlogs. It was just some background shots, for atmosphere."

"You filmed women. Up close. And kept the videos. If you used them anywhere, then show me where. Now!" Connor pushed.

Hayden's defenses were crumbling. He was all out of arguments, Cami saw.

"I know I shouldn't have taken or kept that footage. I'm—I guess you could say—like a voyeur. It makes me feel good to see women using my café like it's their home. I like to zoom in on their expressions. It's innocent, I swear. I'm no killer. I'm a café owner, not a criminal."

"Where were you last night, at about eleven p.m.?"

"I was in my apartment. The café closes at ten."

"Do you have footage of yourself in the apartment with a time stamp?"

Hayden looked embarrassed. "I turn the cameras off after hours."

"Interesting. So, not really for security then," Connor observed as Hayden squirmed. "What about yesterday morning, at around seven a.m.?"

He sighed. "I was in my apartment. The café opens at seven, but I only come through myself an hour or so later."

"And no camera footage?"

"I live alone!" he protested.

"Can anyone confirm that?"

"I'm telling the truth!" Hayden protested, but his back was against a wall now, and he looked beaten.

"What about Tuesday, early evening?"

"I'd need to look back in my diary. Tuesday's my day off. I could have been shopping, or resting, at that time. I might be able to figure it out." He pulled a phone out of his pocket and began scrolling through.

"So you have no real alibi for any of the times of the murders," Connor said.

Cami's mind was racing as she watched him intently. It looked as if this was a strong suspect, for sure. She could see from the set of his shoulders that Connor was now seriously on the offensive. He looked exactly the same as he'd looked before he began reading Cami his rights.

But even though Cami would have liked nothing better than for this sleazy man to be the killer, she realized that there was another box she needed to check. Just in case this slippery man was, in fact, telling the truth when he said he wasn't a killer.

Because, as she watched, she saw he was scrolling using his right hand. That single fact told her that she needed to look further.

"Hayden Mars—" Connor began, his voice booming around the room.

Cami had no doubt that an arrest was going to follow. And if Hayden was arrested and taken in, he couldn't agree to do what she now needed him to do. Now that she'd thought of this possibility, she couldn't ignore it.

"Connor," she pleaded, grabbing his arm. "Please. Wait. There's one more thing I want to find out, first."

CHAPTER TWENTY TWO

Cami knew Connor wouldn't be happy about the delay. She could see he was happy with the evidence. All three victims had spent time in this café shortly before their deaths. The owner had filmed them illicitly and had hidden from the FBI. He was clearly tech-savvy and could have easily found out their addresses and other information.

Connor wanted to push forward, make the arrest, and get this case wrapped up. He wanted the criminal in custody and the killings to be over.

So did she, but not before she'd ruled out this one last possibility.

"What is it?" he asked in frustrated tones.

Striding over to the door, he beckoned her to follow.

"Cami, what's going on? Is this a delaying tactic, are you trying to be clever with this suspect, or is there a genuine reason why you are interrupting me just before we bring him in?"

"There is a genuine reason," she insisted in a whisper. She could see Hayden's curious glance their way. He'd picked up there was conflict between them. Most likely he would be looking to capitalize on it, and she might already have compromised the case by doing that, and given him an advantage he didn't deserve.

"Are you able to explain it? Be quick and use plain English?" Connor sounded impatient.

"Firstly, he's scrolling with his right hand. We're looking for a left-handed killer."

There was a pause. She saw Connor give a reluctant nod.

"Okay. Well observed. Anything else?"

"I do think the fact all three victims were here is too much of a coincidence. But maybe someone else was here, in the café, scouting for victims. Someone who knew this place attracts a lot of people who love online and social media and who came here to hunt."

"Okay?" Connor said dubiously.

"I can't explain it more plainly than that."

"You don't have to. I get you. But how do we pinpoint that person?"

“We need to analyze the technology to see if anyone else was here at all the right times. And none of the wrong times."

Connor sighed. The frown lines in his forehead seemed to deepen.

"Okay," he said. "I acknowledge that's a possibility. And are you able to take it further? Is what you are suggesting going to be doable?"

Cami nodded. “It should be. Especially if he cooperates.”

Connor raised an eyebrow. “Well, then. Let’s see if he will.”

Hurriedly, Cami turned to Hayden.

"I need to access your wi-fi router," she said.

"My router?"

Now he was defensive. He'd sensed that there was conflict between the two people who were targeting him. Cami's interruption had broken the hold that Connor had over him. Now he thought he could get out, free and clear.

"I need to look at it, and see who’s been logging on. I need to go back in your records and search the IP addresses," Cami said.

"Not a chance." He folded his arms. "That's private information."

Connor stepped forward, his heavy face drawn into lines of threat. "You are speaking like a man with a choice," he said conversationally.

Now Hayden looked worried.

"I guess you do have a choice," Connor continued. "You can refuse access to your router, or you can allow it. If you allow it, then this expert can do the research she needs to. You realize this research might clear you?"

"And if I refuse?"

"Then I continue reading your rights, and we bring you in."

There wasn't an inch of give in Connor's demeanor. Not a hint that he wouldn't do exactly as he promised.

And Cami watched Hayden come to the same realization and crumble.

"You want to look at it? Look into it? Sure, okay, if it's those circumstances, I get you," he said. He seemed to be fully on board with the idea, after Connor had said it was the only way for him to escape arrest.

That would make it easy for Cami to assess what she needed to, and to allay—or else confirm—the dark suspicion that was lurking in her mind.

"How long is this going to take?" Connor asked.

"As long as I need to check it," Cami said.

"What do you need?" Hayden demanded. "That you haven't already figured out?" he added, with a rather sour look at her.

"It'll go quicker if you give me all the access codes."

To her surprise, he grabbed a keyboard from a nearby rental laptop, typed in a passcode, and pushed it over to her.

"There. Take it. Just don't delete my business stuff, right? Otherwise, do what you need to."

She could see he was anxious to do anything to avoid trouble. He was embarrassed and seriously worried that he'd been exposed for his sick little hobby of filming clients.

But was he a killer? That was the question.

Or had someone else been using this popular online destination, knowing it was frequented by so many active users who interacted and debated, who criticized and fought?

Cami immediately logged into the wi-fi router and began searching through the files. Opening her laptop, she called up the other information she needed.

This was now a simple process of comparing records. Looking at the times when the victims had been here and been online. Seeing who else had been here and been online at the same time.

And then, the million-dollar question.

Had anyone been here, and been online and watching, when all three of the victims were in this café?

If she could find an IP address in common, that had been here at the right times, then it would mean they had a second suspect, over and above Hayden. Someone who had been sitting here in this dark, trendy, sought-after space with the purpose of targeting victims that he had a desire to kill, and who had been looking into their interactions and gathering information on them.

Cami worked as fast as she could. She knew what a hurry Connor was in, and that she didn't have much time. She had some apps and software that could help speed up the process of searching. She harnessed them all.

This one could help with speedily collating the IPs. This one could help with the comparison.

And this one could help with identifying the common person, if there was such a person to be found.

"I'm getting something," she said. "It looks like there's a common IP address, but I'm just narrowing it down to make sure," she told him. Her software was all working, the numbers scrolling by, the algorithms doing their job. And then, it worked. The computer language was clear, the meaning conclusive.

Just one IP address in common, and in the past few weeks, it had been there during most of Brooke's visits, three of Emma's, and in Cleo's recent visit to this destination.

Someone had been there, waiting and watching. Searching further, Cami saw this IP address had been here a lot in the past few weeks.

And now, the most important information at all.

"Was this IP address here during the murders?" Cami muttered, triangulating the times.

She let out a shaky breath, pushing her shoulders back to release the tension in them.

"He wasn't here at those times," she concluded.

This mystery man, a frequent visitor here, had not been at the Art House Café when any of the murders had been committed. And that told her everything she needed to know.

This person had been here when the victims had been present, but not when the murders had been committed. Her algorithms had run, and there was no other IP address that fitted the same parameters of time.

She thought, at last, they had found the person responsible for these crimes. At any rate, his IP address was now known to them.

But an IP address alone was not enough. They needed an identity to go with it, and fast.

CHAPTER TWENTY THREE

"I need to work on this IP address," Cami muttered. This was so important, and the possibilities were so vast. Pinpointing an IP address was tricky work at the best of times.

Connor had called in two of the local cops to stand guard—one outside the café, and one monitoring Hayden. He was still a suspect, even though their research was pointing to the possibility of somebody else. While the cops stood guard, Cami was working frantically in another secluded corner, on her own machine this time, trying to locate the IP address.

But Connor, impatient with the delay as usual, seemed keen to embark on a feet-on-the-ground approach.

"This customer has been here recently, correct?" Connor asked Cami. Glancing up, she nodded.

"Yes. He's been here in the past couple of weeks, a few times," Cami said. She felt stressed that this person was so near, yet so far. They were sitting here, in the exact place he'd been operating, and yet, they couldn't find him without a struggle.

She opened all her programs and linked up the mapping app.

"Good old-fashioned research might get us further," Connor said. He stood up and headed over to the till. There, the waitress was huddled behind the counter, perched on a stool, looking uncomfortable and uneasy at what was happening in the café.

"Ma'am, what's your name?" Connor asked her.

"Sandi," she said nervously.

"Sandi, we're doing some research. Perhaps you can help us. Do you mind coming over here for a while?" Connor asked.

In a moment, the waitress followed Connor over, walking a few steps behind him, glancing at where Hayden was sitting with the policeman as if worried she was going to be forced to get her boss into trouble.

"We have a situation here, ma'am," Connor said politely. "It won't mean any trouble for you. We are looking to find a customer who has been here frequently. I'd like to know, if we gave you the past few dates and times he's been here, whether you can remember who he is?"

"Sure, I can try," Sandi said, glancing at Hayden again. But her boss was in no mood to put the brakes on this endeavor.

"Whatever they want, help them out," he called, with a slightly desperate tone.

Quickly, Cami looked back at the dates in common with all the victims so that she could give the waitress the times when the IP address had logged in.

"Monday afternoon. Wednesday morning. Thursday morning," she said. “And he was here again yesterday for a few hours, mid-morning to mid-afternoon.”

She felt a cold sensation in her stomach as she realized how much time he’d spent here. How many victims had he managed to find?

"Time frame?" Connor asked calmly.

"He logged on at about ten a.m. And he disconnected at about three p.m."

So yesterday, one of your customers was here most of the day. A regular who often uses this café. We’re looking for a male customer, of above average height and build."

"There are a few customers who come in regularly and stay for long hours," she stated nervously. "There were definitely four or five people here for all of that time yesterday."

"How many men?" Connor quizzed.

"Three, I think," Sandi stammered. “Three regular men who would fit your description. One regular woman, and we had a new customer stay here the whole of yesterday too.”

She was looking very nervous now. Cami hoped she’d be able to give more information. But in the meantime, her programs were running, hunting down that IP address. And finally, she had something. A hint of a direction.

"He lives to the north of here," she said. "A few miles north, probably."

"Does that ring any bells?" Connor asked the waitress. “Do you know where any of the regulars are from?”

"No. I'm sorry, but no."

"Did these customers pay cash? Or card?"

"Most people do pay by card," she said. "Card is definitely the most popular. But there is one guy who pays cash. He was here yesterday."

"What are the names of the two people who use their cards? And the name of the cash payer if you know him?"

Now, Cami saw that Connor was getting out his phone and dialing. Clearly, he was going to call these names through to Ethan, who could run a search on the addresses, and see if any of them linked to the place that she was pinpointing.

"Barry Reese. Colin Avery. And Miles—Miles somebody. He's the one who pays cash."

"Miles lives locally," Hayden offered helpfully. He was looking over toward them, listening intently to as much of their conversation as he could pick up. "Miles lives close by, in an apartment block across the road. I've spoken to him a few times. He walks here, pays cash, works online. He's a copyeditor for travel sites."

"I think we can rule Miles out," Cami said. "That's too close for this triangulation. My IP is showing further north, for sure."

Connor got on the phone.

"Ethan. Two names. Can you check addresses?" He waited, listened.

"We've got Barry Reese and Colin Avery. Both paid by credit card, so you should be able to pull those details."

He waited again. "Right."

Connor sounded slightly disappointed.

"Barry Reese lives on Rose Road, which is a couple miles south of here. And Colin Avery lives west of this café. He lives about eight miles away, on the outskirts of town."

"I'm definitely getting north," Cami insisted. She wasn't wrong. She was sure she was right. North was where this IP address was taking her.

Cami looked at Sandi again.

But to her, this woman was now looking upset. Uncomfortable. She was twisting her fingers together in a conflicted way.

“What is it?” she asked.

The waitress turned her eyes to Cami in appeal.

“Can I ask my boss a question?”

“Sure. Of course,” Cami said, picking up Connor’s subtle nod of agreement.

Raising her voice, Sandi spoke. "Hayden, did you ever actually see Miles's apartment? Or did he just tell you where he lives?"

There was a short silence. Hayden looked surprised.

"He told me. I mean, in conversation. But it made sense. He said that's why he was here so often. Why would I doubt him?"

"Because he told me that he was a website designer who works in e-commerce. Not a travel copyeditor. And that he lives in a guesthouse that his aunt runs."

"He did?" Hayden sounded puzzled.

"Yes. So we're getting different stories from him. Maybe he doesn't live nearby and that was just an excuse for why he's here so often?"

"What impression did this person give you?" Connor asked.

"I'm no expert, but I would have called him a loner," the waitress explained. "He gets here early, and sits at his table with his laptop out. He keeps to himself. He doesn't like to be interrupted and you seldom get chit-chat, but when he feels like talking, it's like he almost commands you to listen. He wears a baseball cap. And he always sits in a corner where you can't see his screen."

"Is he left or right handed?"

"I don't remember."

"Did he ever seem to get angry? Upset?" Cami knew Connor was thinking of how he might have reacted to the social media baiting, assuming he'd been tracking it.

She frowned. "Now that you mention it, yes. He often seemed mad at something. He'd put his head down and type furiously, slam his cup down. Definitely, he'd look like something was making him mad. I always thought he was just having difficulty with his coding."

Cami glared at her programs as if they were letting her down. She still wasn't getting what she needed. They were not allowing her to locate the IP address with enough accuracy in what looked to be a very crowded neighborhood. And they didn't even have Miles's last name.

“Did he ever use his card?” Connor pressed. Turning to the waitress, he spoke in a reasonable and encouraging tone. “Maybe he was caught short, maybe something happened? Even people who routinely pay cash sometimes don’t have it available.”

Sandi tilted her head, and Cami could see she was trying desperately to remember. Sticking her hands under the table, Cami crossed her fingers tightly for a moment.

“You know what,” she said. “I think he did. He might have used his card a week or so ago. He ordered food, and then he didn't have enough cash on him. So he used it. I'm remembering that now. I just don't know exactly when it was. But I can look?"

"Please, look," Connor encouraged. "Go back through the slips and the records, and tell me when you find it."

She hurried back to the till and began searching. The rustling of paper now seemed loud in the otherwise very silent café.

"I think I must have been wrong," she called out, disappointed. "I can't find a Miles at all here. Not on any card."

For a moment, a devastated silence filled the café. But then, Cami had an idea. If this man lied routinely to camouflage his identity, he might have lied about his name too.

“Maybe look for the timing of the bills,” she said. “I can tell you exactly the time his IP address logged out. Perhaps that will match up with a card payment, if he asked for the check soon before he left?”

Cami read out the time, and the waitress looked again.

"You're right," Sandi said, now sounding very confused. "There is one, and it has to be him. I remember he always has this burger. But the card is in the name of Austin Davies."

Cami exchanged an excited glance with Connor.

"I think we’ve got our man," he said.

CHAPTER TWENTY FOUR

It had been a long day yesterday for the tracker, staking out his potential targets. A long day, but a rewarding one. Because he'd ended up with a kill in the evening, and also with the perfect prey for this morning. This was a step forward. In a way, he felt it was a progression.

He was moving on. Becoming bolder.

Hacking in and getting his mind focused had taken more time yesterday, as he'd sat in the atmospheric gloom of the Art House Café, because he'd been feeling overwhelmed by the memories and immediacy of his past experiences. The excitement of the hunt. The exhilaration of the kill. He'd been distracted for a couple of hours by the sheer need for it to happen again. But yesterday's planning had almost gone wrong. While he was distracted, the person he'd been researching for a few days had walked out of the café before he'd been able to grab the final information he needed.

That meant that for a long while yesterday, he'd been unable to find the right person, because nobody else on his shortlist had been available for him to take those final steps that would uncover who they were. But luckily, he'd managed to find the perfect one, just as he was beginning to despair.

It was strange how, a week ago, he'd felt that just one kill would be enough.

But since then, he'd realized how important this mission was. It was something that couldn't be stopped. He couldn't rush it—of course—but he had to continue as fast as he was able to.

So, how to go forward?

He'd done his best. He'd reached out all his tentacles.

And he'd found one woman, who he was now putting the finishing touches to on his home computer. He had her name. He had her address.

Then, he'd had a brief struggle with his own conscience over whether she was the right target. There had been certain elements in her character and background that had made him hesitate. That had given him some pause for thought.

Perhaps she was not as bad as the others. That, he acknowledged, looking at who she was and what she did. But he had to apply his rules equally, and without a doubt, this woman had showed moments of aggression. He'd been alerted when she'd started arguing with someone on an animal rescue page.

"If you dump animals, you're scum. Pure and simple. Scum!"

"It's not dumping if you give them to a shelter."

"It is if you could keep them, but you don't. A shelter is there to help people and animals in need, with no other choices. It isn't there to take your pet because you don't feel like having a dog anymore. If you dump a dog 'just because,' you are the lowest, most dreadful person, scum of humanity, and you deserve the worst!"

He could see the vitriol lurking in her words. This woman was vicious, for sure. She was the mold that he was looking for. He could see the capacity for cruelty there. It was surging close to the surface, just itching to be unleashed.

She was arguing with intensity. She was crushing her opponent. And he hated her for that, even if it took a bit of mental agility to hate her for this particular argument. But he hardened his heart. This woman deserved to die.

She would be an excellent choice for his next kill.

The fact that this woman seemed to be doing good in the world was not important. If he started taking every case on the merits of the person involved, it would get far too complicated. That was not up to him to judge.

He was just there to remove them from society when they started their aggression.

Memories surged inside him, unwanted memories that he would rather have forgotten.

His sister's face swum into his mind. Beautiful, but vulnerable. Damaged. Always weak, always fragile. Years ago, at the age of twenty, she'd taken her life.

He never knew why. Never knew the reasons. But as time went on, and he became exposed more and more to the horrors of the online world, it was as if he had an epiphany.

Of course it was because of these nameless, faceless online bullies. That must have been the reason for it. Why else would there have been no clear explanation for that tragedy? Sure, he knew they'd had a bad family life, a bad upbringing, but he'd always taken care of her. It was only when she was grown that she'd been exposed to the cruelty in the world.

It had felt like a light going on in his brain, and from that moment he had known that it was his mission to save others. The weak, the downtrodden, the ones who could not fight for themselves.

He would fight for them.

It started with his sister's death, after all. If she had just been protected from the harshness of life, she might still be here today. If people fought online—no matter the reason—he was going to be there, ready to give them payback.

Their character didn't matter. It was by their actions that he was judging them. Now, he had his new target, and he was excited.

All that was necessary was to put the finishing touches to his research. He had almost everything he needed. And, as his fingers flew over the keys in his tiny, cramped home office, he was able to amend that with the final piece of information.

He had everything he needed. He was now armed and ready to take this woman down.

Was she online? She would need to be.

He checked, knowing he needed that window to get to her, that he needed the world to know what he'd done through that stark and final statement. Typing it on the victims' keyboards always felt immensely satisfying as if carefully laid plans were unfolding in exactly the way they should.

It was such poetic justice.

There was her most commonly used page. Yes, she was online. She was interacting. And from what she was busy with, he saw it would give him enough time to get to her place. He remembered the layout, where the doors and windows were. He was pretty sure she'd be in her upstairs study. That was where he expected to find her.

He checked that his blade was sharp and put his gloves in his pocket. His fingers were trembling very slightly as he touched the hard and lethally sharp steel, and with a sense of wonderment, he realized the feeling was excitement. That was what he felt now. Like a runner before a race, pumped, tense, and ready. The fear he'd felt during the first times had faded completely, and now he was surprised that he'd ever felt that way.

It was like a secret that only he knew about.

That same feeling he'd had when smoking an illicit cigarette behind his house, where his parents were shouting and screaming at each other, and he was skipping school. He couldn't think of a better way to describe it, this weird, yet incredibly addictive rush that was surging through him right now.

He understood the power of his position, and the importance of his new role. That this was his calling in life. A vocation to kill those that took their anger at the world and spread it through words, destroying people they didn't even know. This was no different than writing a novel, or drawing pictures on a computer. It was an expression of his new-found freedom and power.

He climbed into the car. He had everything he needed. His map software, spare gloves, a towel to wipe his blade, a bag to stash any stained clothing, and a change of clothes.

A bottle of water and a few refresher towels in case he needed to clean up afterwards. Everything was thought out and nothing left to chance. He was familiar with every mile of the journey, having run through it many times on maps and in street view.

Cold, calm, and sure, his route was mapped out and he felt certain about every step of the way.

The minutes were ticking down, and in twenty more of them, his target would die.

CHAPTER TWENTY FIVE

Austin Davies was their man, Cami felt sure of it. He'd been present—and absent—at exactly the right times, and it was clear his own timing had aligned with the victims'. And now, they were racing north to find him.

Huddled in the passenger seat, juggling her devices, she was getting every scrap of information she could find on this suspected killer.

Local cops had been called in to hold Hayden and secure the scene until they were totally sure that they were pursuing the right man. Connor hadn't wanted one suspect to sneak away while they were on the trail of another, even if that one seemed stronger. So he'd explained to Cami, as they had rushed downstairs together and headed for the car.

Meanwhile, Connor was on the radio, going back and forth with Ethan, who was linked up to all the FBI databases. Information was filtering through, narrowing down his location even as they sped to the area.

"He's got a recorded address that I've found," Ethan announced triumphantly. With lights flashing, they were powering forward toward the densely populated residential area where Austin lived.

"What is it?" Connor glanced at the map on his satnav.

"He's at 414 Exeter Heights," Ethan said. "Corner of Willow and Main."

"Got it," Connor said calmly, swerving past a slower car and accelerating so fast that Cami's stomach was left behind. Quickly, she grabbed her laptop tighter.

"Any criminal record?"

"Nope. No record. But I looked back further."

Cami felt a spark of admiration for Ethan's work ethic. He wasn't a quitter. She liked that he would take things a few more steps in the search for the full picture.

"Find anything?"

"Yes. His father has a record. He spent four years in jail for assault," Ethan said excitedly. "And there's other weird stuff too. It seems Austin's mother disappeared when he was twenty years old under suspicious circumstances. And two years later, his younger sister committed suicide."

"Thanks for the background," Connor said. “It might be relevant.”

Cami thought it was very relevant.

"I think this guy fits the profile," Connor said in a matter-of-fact voice, although Cami could see the tension on his face. "That family history, that troubled past, is an important factor."

Cami's gut feeling told her the same thing. Now, all they had to do was get to him to confirm what they both believed. Connor kept his eyes front, hands on the steering wheel, concentrating on the road like a race driver.

Ethan's voice came again over the radio.

"I can't find a cell number for him," he said, sounding disappointed. "There's one on record, but it seems to be out of service."

"I can," Cami said, glancing at her screen. "I've found something online, and it looks like it's current."

"Did you get that?" Connor asked Ethan. "We have one."

Quickly, Cami read it out. She felt a sense of triumph in having located a phone number for this man.

"He's a part-time programmer," she said. "He writes software for a living. Without a doubt, he knows how to hack. And that's what he must have been doing in that café. Choosing victims, getting a visual ID, logging in, spying on their interactions, then tracking them down in real life."

The method was chilling in its effectiveness.

"Let's not jump to conclusions," Connor warned. "First things first, we need to get face to face with him."

"You want me to come through?" Ethan said.

"No. Not yet. We might still need you that side. But be ready."

Cami could hear the tension thrumming in Connor's voice as they swung onto Main Street and sped down.

This was a quirky area of town, with high-rise apartments, food stalls, and restaurants with a spread of street cuisine that seemed to represent every continent and artful murals painted on sometimes crumbling walls.

Connor stopped outside a tall, shabby looking apartment block.

"This is it," he said. "This is where our suspect lives. Now, let's get up to number 414 and find him."

Exeter Heights looks like it has seen better days, Cami thought as she bundled her laptop back in the bag and shoved it under the seat, grabbing her phone before jumping out. It was an elderly, six-story building with a shabby frontage.

Apartment 414 was on the fourth floor. In the lobby, where one small and elderly camera was positioned on the far wall, there was no sign of any attendant or security. Connor rushed to the elevator and pressed the button for the fourth floor.

After waiting for a couple of seconds as the elevator creaked and groaned, seemingly without budging from its position on the fifth floor, Connor shook his head impatiently.

"We don't have time to waste. Let's take the stairs."

He pushed open the side door, and a smell of damp and diesel rushed out from the parking garage below. Then, Connor powered up the stairs, his legs working tirelessly as he headed for the floor they needed.

Cami rushed behind him, bursting through the door onto the fourth floor, which was in slightly better shape than street level with some repairs done to the tiling and a few tired looking planters set along the corridor.

What would happen in this confrontation? she wondered. *Would Austin be violent?* Her stomach twisted as she thought about what could play out.

Connor's hand dropped instinctively to his gun for a moment as he approached the door, as if reassuring himself it was at the ready, and she knew he was thinking the same. Then he lifted a hand and knocked loudly on the door.

There was no answer from inside. Just a silence that stretched uneasily out.

Connor knocked again while Cami prowled down the corridor. Here was a window. She peeked through it and narrowed her eyes, peering through a gap in the blinds.

She could see the shape of a computer screen, mounted on the wall.

"I'm only getting a glimpse of it, but it seems he has quite an IT setup here," she said.

Connor knocked again. But Cami was sure now that Austin Davies was not going to answer. Was he hiding away inside? Or was he somewhere else?

"What if he's gone to target somebody?" she asked in a small voice. "What if he spent yesterday at the café, doing his research, and he's ready to kill again today?"

"It's a possibility," Connor agreed, his voice hard.

He got on the phone.

"Ethan? Can you track that number for me? We need a live location on it."

"Sure. The one you gave me earlier?"

"Yes. That one."

There was a pause.

"I can't do it," Ethan said, disappointed. "Phone's turned off. Or out of range, but there aren't many dead spots in Boston, so off would be my guess."

"Thanks," Connor said heavily, cutting the call.

"What can we do? Can you break in?" Cami said, feeling anxious at being so thoroughly checkmated. They were standing right outside his house! Right outside! But he wasn't here and they couldn't track him.

"I can't do that. There's not enough cause as yet."

"Not enough cause?" Her frustrations with the FBI surged all over again, but with an effort, she bit back her feelings. This was not the time and in any case, Connor sounded as if, for a moment, he also deeply resented the rules he had to work within.

Could she get into his network? Cami tried to access the network in the apartment. But it, too, was tightly locked down. She might be able to do it, but not in a minute. This was more like an hour's job.

And then, another idea flickered into her mind.

"Connor, if he was searching for victims yesterday, what about checking out the two women who were at the café all day? Remember, the waitress said there were two women and three men there most of the day? If he was tracking a suspect, it might be one of these women. We could even take a look online and see if they acted in a way that might have triggered him."

"Now that's a good idea," Connor said.

He picked up his phone again, and this time, he dialed the local cops who were at the café.

"We need information from the waitress," he said. "The two female customers she mentioned, who were at that café yesterday. We need their names, and any other details."

"Two female customers? Let me ask," the cop said.

The short wait felt interminable. Cami paced up and down the corridor, fidgeting. Every so often, she checked the program she was running to try and gain access to Austin's home network, but so far, there was no progress. Zero. She couldn't have felt more frustrated.

And then, Connor spoke again, looking at Cami.

"We have two names from their card payments. Anne Goode and Fifi Easton. I'm going to get addresses from Ethan now, but if one of them has done anything to trigger him, we need to know. How fast can you work?"

CHAPTER TWENTY SIX

Anne Goode. Fifi Easton. Having names made them feel real, human, fragile, and vulnerable. Standing right there in the corridor, outside the suspected killer's apartment, Cami went hunting online, only vaguely aware that Connor was snapping out instructions to Ethan.

Their behavior online would be the deciding factor, and the element that might have caught the killer's attention.

She researched Fifi Easton first.

There didn't seem to be much to find on Fifi Easton, Cami realized, feeling disappointed. She seemed like a solid citizen, not the same profile as the others. She was an accountant, who did work for a few private clients and also for a few charities and good causes.

"What are you getting?" Connor asked impatiently. Now it was his turn to pace, while Cami hunted.

"Not much," she said. "From her resume, she does accounting work for a few clients and one or two charities." That didn't sound like something that would trigger a killer's ire. "I'm going to look up the other woman now."

Leaving a few searches running for Fifi, just in case anything else came up, Cami turned her attention to Anne Goode.

"Let's go downstairs while you search," Connor said. "If we're in the car and ready to go, it will save time." He got on the phone to Ethan again as he strode back down the corridor.

"Send me geolocations for the two addresses of these victims," he said. "And do another check on Austin's cellphone. Perhaps it’s traceable now."

Following him downstairs, Cami almost tripped over the tiles on the landing, she was so focused on her phone.

Anne Goode. Who was she. Surely Anne had done something to rile Austin? Surely there must be an obvious finger pointing in one direction?

Anne Goode was far more active on social media. She was in marketing. She worked for a few big firms, as well as for a shelter for abused women, and this drew Cami's attention immediately. If you ran a shelter for battered women, you might end up lashing out online.

She had a lot of friends, and it was through her social activity that Anne seemed to interact with the world.

Had she said something wrong and triggered the killer? Had he been stalking her online?

"Connor, I think I've found something," Cami said, aware that her excitement had ratcheted up afresh. "Anne seems to use social media more. She's in marketing, but she has plenty to say outside of it too. She gets into a few arguments that I've seen so far."

It wasn't the same level of vitriol and taunting that she'd noticed on the other victims' pages, and that worried her slightly. But without a doubt, Anne would have attracted his attention by being outspoken and engaging with a variety of people while not being scared to voice her views.

Was she correct, though? There was so much riding on this. What if she was wrong?

"I think it's Anne," Cami said. It had to be Anne.

"Anne. Right. We're going there now." Connor sped up his pace as he rushed down the final flight of stairs.

Cami followed, still feeling conflicted, and as if there was something she might be missing. But what could it possibly be? They had a fairly likely victim who interacted and was vocal online regularly. She spoke her mind and it wasn't always what people wanted to hear.

"Ethan? What's Anne Goode's address?" Connor asked.

"Looking it up now," he replied calmly. A moment later, he spoke again.

"It's 33 Crystal Road. Eight miles south of where you are now."

"We're going there. Meet me there. We can use you now. You got a cellphone number for this woman?"

"I've got her business phone, yes."

"I'm going to warn her."

But as Connor was dialing, Cami scrambled into the car, still glued to her phone, and she realized what she was missing.

"Connor!" she said loudly. "Wait!"

"What?" Now, he sounded anxious. "What now? Are we wrong?"

"She's not there!" Cami felt breathless. It had taken her far too long to do the simple job of looking at Anne Goode's upcoming bookings and engagements. "Today, she's out of state. She flew to San Francisco early this morning to organize a function there. So there's no way he can be targeting her."

"You think he would have known?" Connor asked.

"I'm telling you, yes. Absolutely one hundred percent yes. He would have known. He researches his victims very, very carefully."

"It's the other one then, I guess? Only you said she doesn't interact much? Would she have done enough to trigger him? We may be on the totally wrong track here. He might be chasing after someone else."

"I'm double checking. Wait!" Cami's breath caught in her throat. She'd just found what she needed.

Fifi Easton did all the accounts work for an animal shelter that she was clearly passionate about. She even helped the shelter load new adoptable animals on their website and social media. And although she didn't say much online outside of this, Cami saw that yesterday had been an exception.

Yesterday, uncharacteristically, Fifi had exploded, triggered by a man who'd said that shelters should accept any unwanted animals and that people were entitled to dump their pets there if they didn't want to keep them anymore. She had retaliated in similar form to Brooke, Cleo, and Emma. She'd given him a piece of her furious mind.

She had pretty much destroyed him.

"If you dump animals, you're scum. Pure and simple. Scum!"

"It's not dumping if you give them to a shelter."

"It is if you could keep them, but you don't. A shelter is there to help people and animals in need, with no other choices. It isn't there to take your pet because you don't feel like having a dog anymore. If you dump a dog 'just because,' you are the lowest, most dreadful person, scum of humanity, and you deserve the worst!"

And even though Cami was one hundred percent on Fifi's side, and didn't know how anyone could find fault with what she said, she acknowledged that a killer didn't think logically. The argument itself might have been enough for him. Especially if he'd been looking out for an excuse. He'd been seeking a target.

Fifi was the one who'd triggered him. She must have been.

"Austin is on that group also," she said, feeling tension fill her as she checked the community group's membership. "He joined yesterday. He must have seen that she was a member and logged in to see if she fit his profile. And it just so happened that yesterday, she let it rip in a totally uncharacteristic way. We need to get to her, Connor. He could be there already."

"She lives twenty miles out!" Connor said in disgust. "All the way out of town on a smallholding. It's going to take us half an hour to get there."

"Warn her," Cami pleaded.

"We'll try," Connor said, pulling away with a squeal of tires and powering towards the highway. Cami heard the edge of tension in his voice and felt it keenly.

Ethan's voice came over the radio.

"I got Fifi's number. It's current—seems to be, anyway. But she's not picking up."

Cami felt her stomach clench. Her imagination was running ahead, taking her all the way to that grisly sight of the bodies in the morgue. Not another, she prayed. Surely not another. She couldn't bear to think that they might arrive too late—perhaps by just a few minutes—to see this woman lying there like the others, her life taken by those deep, sharp slashes. How would she feel if that happened? Cami didn't want to think about it. But she had to keep fighting, keep trying. Surely there was still something she could do?

"I'll see if I can find another number. Maybe she has more numbers, maybe there's a super-private one."

She knew it was a vain hope, but she went searching all the same.

They were running out of time. Wherever Fifi Easton was, whatever she was doing right now, Cami felt sure that Austin was either on his way to her or had already arrived.

Fifi might already be dead. But, if she was still alive, she had no idea of the extent of danger she was in.

CHAPTER TWENTY SEVEN

It was time for her to die.

He walked down the road that led to Fifi Easton's house, taking in the unusual setting. So far, his kills had all been in urban areas. This was a more rural setting. The house was set on a small plot of land, about an acre in size, backed by farms.

The house had a tiny attic that had been converted to an office, nothing more than a wooden platform that seemed to have been built as an afterthought. This was where Fifi worked. His research had shown him that.

She had a husband, but he was away. He was a helicopter pilot who often flew on overnight trips. No doubt, Fifi thought she was safe without him in this quiet rural setting.

He smiled as he climbed out of the car, closing the door quietly. The car was “hidden in plain sight” as best as he could. He'd seen a country club down the road and had parked it in there. Being a place filled with rural charm and an air of quiet calmness, he hadn’t expected it to be bristling with cameras and had identified none in the immediate area when he'd searched online earlier. Now he saw that was correct. There were in fact no cameras and that meant he could park there without being noticed or seen.

He was breathing hard. This time, there wasn't the faintest flicker of fear in his mind, but only a keen edge of anticipation. He could not wait to do what he needed to. To take her life. This woman who had been so cruel, so condemning online yesterday.

As he paced down the road, wearing a blue jacket and tracksuit pants because he wanted to fit in with the “countryside” ethos, and he didn't want anyone to look twice at him, he stared around.

There was a shelter on the left. "Animal Rescue Organization," the sign read. He guessed that was the reason for the big fight and debate she'd had yesterday. She'd been defending the shelter where she helped out.

How apt that he was now walking past what would be, in a short time, the reason for her death.

He smiled. The expression felt cold on his face and unfamiliar. But he thought that if he continued on this mission, he might end up smiling a lot more. Because one thing was for sure, these kills were bringing him what he could only describe as a fierce, destructive joy.

Her door was a simple one, and his toolkit would force it easily. He imagined how surprised she would be when she heard the sound of it being forced. Out here in the country, she wouldn't imagine it possible that anyone could break in.

This woman had no idea who he was—or what she was playing with when she attacked her opponent viciously online yesterday.

Fifi Easton. A middle-aged woman—his oldest victim so far. She had blonde hair streaked with gray and a face that told him she'd had a hard life. Her best feature, without a doubt, was her blue eyes—pale and intense.

He couldn't wait to look into them. But then, she would turn and run, like all the others did. She would flee him, and he would be able to deliver the killing blows.

It was a simple process, but not easy. To stab a blade so hard into a living victim took skill and resolve. In its own way, it was art, he decided. There was great beauty in it. And he reveled in it. For so many years, he'd operated mostly in the online world himself as a programmer. It felt like freedom, now, to be moving in the real world and making such an impact. Delivering justice and balance with each journey he made. Taking those who deserved it.

He took a deep breath and kept walking, picking up his pace as he approached her house. Quickly, he glanced around, making sure that there was nobody watching.

His phone was turned off. He didn't want his presence advertised when he was close by his victims. Locations could be tracked. It would be very stupid to do such a thing, and he wasn't stupid. He planned ahead for everything.

But then, there was an unexpected hitch.

He saw a woman jogging down the road in his direction with her dog on a leash. He hesitated for only a moment. Smoothly, as if he'd never intended to turn through Fifi's garden gate at all, he kept walking. This was just a tiny blip on the radar. He'd had similar moments before, where he'd had to delay a minute and wait for the right time.

But to his dismay, as he walked on, the approaching woman smiled, giving him a breathless greeting as she jogged closer.

"Isn't it a great morning? So warm. Or maybe it's just me!" Falling back into a walk, she wiped perspiration from her forehead. The dog made a bee-line for him, wagging its tail. He stepped back in consternation, not wanting this engagement, but then he remembered the role he was playing. He smiled, patted the dog's head, and beamed at this sweaty, brunette, thirty-something woman in her running pants and trainers as if it was the best experience of his entire life to meet her.

"It is warm," he said. It had been a mistake to come out here. He'd anticipated everything. Absolutely everything—except the human factor and the increased friendliness of country folk. That, he hadn't accounted for, and now it was about to bite him, because she had seen him closely and might remember and recognize him.

"Well, enjoy your walk."

"And enjoy your run," he smiled.

"It's over, thank goodness. I only run when my boyfriend goes to work early. Otherwise, we walk together! Time to get ready for work."

Veering to the left, the chatty woman and the dog walked toward a small cabin set in the trees, directly opposite Fifi's house.

The woman opened the cabin's door and stepped inside. She hadn't unlocked it, or locked it again behind her, he noticed. She had no reason to be suspicious. She was just being a good neighbor, having a friendly conversation with someone out for a stroll.

But her neighborliness, her interference, had scuppered his plans.

He should go. His heart thudded with disappointment. It wasn't going to be possible to do this kill. Not after this interaction. Not after being seen so closely. Undoubtedly, the police would interview this nosy woman, and she would say that she'd seen him out on the road and walking past the target's house.

Unless . . . unless . . . he could do things differently.

And with that idea in mind, a plan came to the killer. A plan so elegant that he felt briefly overwhelmed by it. The speed of his own thinking was impressive. He was nimble and agile, able to think on his feet, even in these challenging circumstances. His abilities were growing. He was becoming more and more the person he'd always dreamed of being.

She was alone in the house, and her boyfriend wasn't home.

She was a witness, but she needn't be a witness for long. She was only going to be able to speak to the police for as long as she was alive and breathing.

This could represent a whole new phase in his mission.

He could kill Fifi, and then he could move across the road, fast and lethal, and he could take this interfering neighbor down as she was preparing for work. Grab her as she was putting on make-up or getting out of the shower.

The boldness and audacity of his thinking dazzled him. It spoke volumes about how far he'd come that he was able to think this through with cool logic and without hesitation or squeamishness at all.

The simplicity of the solution was perfect.

Quickly, gripping his knife, he retraced his steps and headed swiftly up the path to Fifi's front door.

CHAPTER TWENTY EIGHT

This was a matter of life and death. Cami felt breathless with tension as they raced to the home of their suspected target.

"I know he's there. I know he is," Cami said, her fingers flying over the keys as she looked for alternative phone numbers for Fifi. "It all adds up. The time they spent at the café yesterday, the fact that he joined that group so recently, the fact that he's not home, and his phone is off."

"We have to keep calm," Connor said, his hands gripping the wheel. "It could be that Austin is somewhere else. He might not be targeting her at all. Let's not create a worst-case scenario before it happens."

But from the flat tone of his words, Cami could hear that he thought the worst case was all too likely.

"How far is it?" she asked.

"Ten minutes. I've called the local police, remember. They might get there sooner."

"But they might not. It's too long," she agonized. She felt sick to her stomach and yet cold at the same time. She felt as if this was her responsibility. That if she could make the right choices, she could prevent another attack from happening.

"Cami?" Ethan's voice, over the radio.

He was speaking to her?

"What?" she asked.

"Just a suggestion, but maybe her phone is on silent. Maybe she's one of those that turns it off when she's working. And if that's the case, why not try to get hold of her in other ways?"

"Other ways? You mean, online?"

"Yes. Perhaps that'll be quicker. Text her. Email her. Tag her on whatever social media she's active on. Remember that if he's there, going to her house, he's confirmed she is online. That's his MO, right? Maybe you can do something there."

"Ethan, that's brilliant!"

In her haste and panic to hack a different phone number, Cami hadn't thought of the calmly logical step that Ethan was now suggesting.

"I'm going to do that straight away," she said.

Where was this woman interacting now? Cami was pretty sure it would be the shelter's social media. That was where she spent most time online. It seemed that updating the available animals for adoption and answering the public's questions was all part of her commitment to helping this place out.

She went to the shelter's homepage, and sure enough, she saw Fifi was hard at work there. She seemed to be uploading the week's intake of new kittens and puppies. Cute and furry canine and feline faces filled the screen. Fifi had a good patter and was clearly an expert at her job, which was basically trying to sell the individual looks and personality of each rescue animal.

Cami had a soft heart when it came to animals. And her tireless work here proved to her that Fifi was truly a good person. She'd had a moment online, that was all. And a moment had been enough as the killer spread his dark wings and looked for new prey.

Now, what could she do? How could she alert Fifi?

There was a message option. Using it, you could message the shelter and talk to someone in real time. Since Fifi was currently online, perhaps she would end up being the go-to.

Cami tried it, pressing the "Connect" button.

"Five minutes away," Ethan's voice intruded on her focus.

For a few moments, nothing happened. But then a chat screen popped up.

"Hi there. Can I help?" That was an automatic message.

"Is that Fifi?" Cami typed, nearly banging her head against the side of the car as Connor swung it around a tight bend.

There was a surprised pause. "Yes. How can I help?"

Words were crucial now, Cami knew. And probably, the best way to do this was the spoken word.

"I've been trying to call you. It's urgent. Are you near your phone?

"Sorry, no. I'm working upstairs. My phone's in the lounge, charging."

Upstairs was safer. Further away from the killer. Going downstairs would expose her more directly to Austin, who could be breaking through her front door at any moment. It was totally the wrong decision. She needed to stay where she was.

"Wait, please. Don't go get it. There's something I need to tell you," Cami typed.

Her words glowed on the screen.

There was no response, and Cami drew in a shaky, scared breath, because she figured out now that the worst had happened.

Fifi had immediately gone downstairs to get her phone.

What she'd done might have killed the woman, and she felt panic flare anew. It was too late, and she had made the wrong decision, and now she didn't know how she could ever live with herself.

But then, a trilling noise filled the car.

She was calling her! Fifi had gotten her phone from downstairs and was calling!

Cami grabbed up the call.

"Fifi?"

"Yes, hon. What is it? My phone is almost dead. It's off the charger now, so I might only have a moment to speak." She sounded brisk, slightly hoarse in tone, and impossibly normal. She was an ordinary, good hearted, innocent woman who had no idea she was in desperate danger. Cami's heart twisted as she heard her voice.

"Please, get to safety. Lock yourself in somewhere. The bathroom, maybe. Wherever has the most solid door," Cami implored her.

"What?" Fifi sounded a mix of disbelieving and incredulous. "Why?"

Would she even believe Cami if she told her she was FBI? Right now, Cami wasn't sure. She didn't know if Fifi would believe her. She might think it was a prank call. She needed to find another way. A more direct way.

A picture, Cami decided. She needed to paint a picture in this woman's mind. The point, right now, was shock value and to spur Fifi into action. In this life-or-death scenario, the most important thing was to get enough locked doors between Fifi and the killer to allow them time to arrive. Every second that she could buy for Fifi now might help.

"I'm from law enforcement. There's a man with a knife outside your front door," she said, breathlessly.

"Hang on, what? How do you know that?"

"It's just been called in."

There was pure disbelief in Fifi's voice, but Cami gripped at it, using it as a lifeline to save the woman's life. "He's lurking outside your home and looking for a way to get in, right now. Please, listen to me. We're on our way. Just do what you can. Get somewhere safe.

Your front door won't be enough. Get behind another door you can lock, and please, do it fast." Cami's tone was imploring. Her breath was rapid, stressed.

But at last, she heard a reluctant sigh of assent.

"Well, I guess, seeing you saw him, I'll—" she began.

And then, Cami's blood chilled as she heard the noise she'd dreaded. A rending, ripping, metallic sound. It could mean only one thing.

Austin was there. He was breaking in.

She heard Fifi scream. And then, silence. The phone battery had died.

And they were still two minutes away.

CHAPTER TWENTY NINE

"No!" Cami clenched her hands together, tears filling her eyes. This was the most horrific scenario she'd ever imagined. She had been listening—actually listening—as the killer had broken in. What she'd heard was a woman's last moments on earth before that sharp, slashing knife blade did its work.

She glanced appealingly at Connor, whose face was stone. "He's got her! He's got her!"

It was all her worst fears brought to life. It was what she dreaded had happened to Jenna. And it was her own fault, because she'd made Fifi go downstairs. If she hadn't gone, if she'd stayed upstairs, then surely she would have been safer?

Connor's hands were welded to the wheel. The road was flying by in a blur. He pulled out to pass another car, hitting the gas so hard that the car fishtailed as it sped.

Above the shrilling of the siren she heard his voice, surprisingly steady.

"Don't think about it, Cami. You need to focus on what we will do when we get there. You did your best. You could not have done more."

Although the words provided cold comfort, they allowed Cami to get a fragile grip on her emotions. She hung onto that resolve doggedly. Connor was right. What happened next was important.

And she was going to make this killer pay. Whatever it took, she was going to make sure that this time, he didn't get away.

"This is the road," Connor said. "She's three farms down." They were driving into the treed, forested countryside. She focused on the end point. It was time. They were here.

She gasped as she saw the front door of the modest wooden house was splintered, hanging open and askew.

Brakes squealed as Connor stopped outside. He jumped out, grasping his gun, and rushed to the house. Cami hastily unfastened her seatbelt and rushed up to the ruined door behind him.

It was terrifying beyond her wildest dreams to be going into a house where a killer waited, and even though she desperately wanted to avenge Fifi, Cami's limbs felt wobbly, and she was breathless with fright. It was as if the scene was playing out in slow motion. As if her legs were taking her straight into deadly danger, but she couldn't turn back.

"FBI!" Connor yelled, bursting through the doorway.

And then, from inside, she heard an enraged roar. The sound was spine-chilling, primal. He was in there.

A gunshot rang out, and she heard a loud crash. With her breath gasping in her throat, she raced the last few yards to the door.

Inside, in the cabin's living room, Connor was grappling with another man, whose back was toward her. This was hard, brutal street fighting, and he must have gotten Connor’s gun away from him. Perhaps it had fallen under a chair or a table, because it was nowhere in sight.

The other man was lean, tall, wiry, and most probably twenty years younger than Connor. It was clear that he was lethally strong, and Connor was barely holding his own. Cami heard boots scuffing on floorboards and the grunts and gasps as they battled together.

Then, hissing in a horrified breath, Cami saw the killer still had the knife. Her blood ran cold as she saw the flashing blade. Connor had hold of his wrist and was using all his strength to keep the other man from slicing that blade down into his neck.

He had no gun, and he was up against an adversary whose only aim was to kill.

The killer lunged forward, swiping his knife down in a swift arc, aiming for Connor's chest. Connor pulled away, but only just in time. He aimed a kick that partially connected. The other man twisted away before resuming his attack. Cami saw the brute strength in his arm as he slashed forward.

She had to help!

Even though she felt like turning and running, Cami crept inside, looking around for any weapon, anything she could use.

There was a fire iron by the fireplace to the right. She guessed that was going to be the best thing to use. There didn't seem to be anything else she could see.

With her heart accelerating, she grabbed the iron, took a deep breath, and rushed forward. She raised it and brought it down, aiming for the killer's head, hoping that she might knock him out.

But, as the blow came down, the man shifted, and the iron glanced off the shoulder.

He hissed out a painful breath and whipped around.

Cami saw his face, a snarl of rage in his eyes, dark and intense and with a glittering madness in them.

And then, with a yell, his arm came up and Cami realized that he was now going to attack her. A vicious roundhouse kick from him brought Connor briefly to his knees, and then she was in the killer's sights.

He lunged, coming at her with the blade slicing through the air.

Cami swung once more, using the fire iron in total desperation.

This time, she got lucky. By pure chance—because she thought she might have closed her eyes as it came down—it connected with his knife hand. She felt a surge of triumph as the fire iron thumped directly down onto his fingers.

He let out a bellow of rage, but he didn’t drop the knife. It only slowed him for a moment, and then he lunged for her again.

Behind him, she saw Connor make a desperate grab for him, and then, there was no more time for anything.

She turned and ran, heading out of the house, her feet pounding over the grass as she raced to the car. He was right behind her. Cami could hear his fast, heavy footfalls. She had to get away. She squeaked with terror as she felt the blade slash at her jacket. It ripped the fabric, but thanks to a desperate swerve, the knife didn’t cut her.

He was going to try again, though. Knowing this, she ran for all she was worth, stumbling over the uneven grass.

With a twist of terror, Cami realized she wasn't going to make it to the car. He was going to grab her before she could reach it. Behind her, she could hear Connor's warning cry.

Connor was rushing to help, but he was too far away, and the killer would reach her first.

The shock of the realization numbed her. She skidded on the dewy grass, fear flaring inside her. In a few more steps he'd reach her and then this was it. This was the end.

Unless there was something she could do. Connor had said to stay calm. To think calmly. She didn't know anything about tactics. All she had was the experience of gaming. And gaming wasn't like real life.

But perhaps in a way, it was, Cami thought.

Gaming was all about speed and resourcefulness and using what you had available. Gaming was about brainpower and skill, doing something different and unexpected, outwitting the bad guys.

She knew what she had available. She knew what she would do now, to save herself, if this was a game. It wasn't much, but perhaps she could make it work.

Cami turned, and flung the fire iron at his head with all her strength.

CHAPTER THIRTY

Cami knew that the fire iron wouldn't be enough to stop this deranged man who was hell bent on killing her. But it did what she hoped it would do.

He raised his hands, dropping the knife, instinctively shielding his face to protect himself from the flying object.

And as he did that, Cami put the second part of her plan into action. She dove for his legs and grabbed onto them as tightly as she could, feeling a flare of pain as his foot caught her in her thigh.

He stumbled forward and sprawled to the ground. Another kick got her in the arm and she gasped in pain, wriggling out of the way before he could grab her again.

And then, Connor was there. He leaped onto the man with such force that Cami literally heard the breath whoosh out of the other man as his knee landed in his back.

A moment later, with frightening efficiency, he'd gotten the handcuffs off his belt and was cuffing the gasping, choking, winded killer.

Sirens wailed, and a local police car arrived, speeding up to the scene. The backup that Ethan had summoned was here.

Voices shouted, and she heard the crackle of radios as two police officers jumped out and rushed over. They took one of the killer's arms each and hauled him to his feet. The man was still struggling violently, but with his hands behind his back and two cops holding him, Cami knew that this was over. He was caught.

"Are you okay?" Connor asked. He reached out a hand and helped her to stand. He was disheveled and still gasping for breath, his jacket was torn, and there was a trickle of blood down his neck.

"I'm okay," she said.

"That was good work. If you're ready, come on. Quick."

He turned toward the wooden house and headed purposefully back toward it.

Fifi! Where was she?

Anxiety flared in Cami all over again as she hurried after him. She hadn't seen the woman's body inside—but there hadn't been time to see much. Was there a chance she'd survived?

Connor walked into the house and this time, Cami had the chance to take a better look around.

The lower part of the cabin consisted of a small living room, now with furniture knocked over and a vase smashed thanks to the struggle. From the living room, a wooden staircase led up to the higher level. That was where Fifi had been working. She saw a desk and a chair.

But a desk, chair, and computer were all there was room for on that small upper level. It was nothing more than a cubbyhole with no doors beyond.

If she'd been there when he'd broken in, Cami realized, feeling stunned, that she would have been trapped and killed instantly. Because upstairs, there was nowhere to go. Coming down had saved her.

Downstairs, beyond the living room, there were two wooden doors.

Both were closed. But one was partially splintered, with kick marks at the base. He'd been trying to force his way to her and had almost gotten in.

"Ma'am?" Connor called, pacing toward the damaged door. He rapped on the wood. "Ma'am, are you there? FBI here. We've arrested your attacker."

Feeling she should also say something, Cami called out, "It's all okay. I spoke to you just now. We got the guy with the knife."

There was only silence and again, she had the terrible feeling they were too late.

But then, her heart skipped as she heard the sound of a key in the lock. The wooden door opened a crack, and Fifi looked out, her graying hair disheveled, her blue eyes wide and scared. But she looked unharmed. She was okay. That vicious knife blade hadn't reached her.

"I'm so glad you're okay," Cami blurted out, feeling relief wash over her.

She was alive but looked utterly shocked and unsteady on her feet as though she might collapse. Connor took her arm and gently guided her over to the closest chair.

"You sit there, ma'am," he told her with surprising gentleness in his voice. "Can I bring you some water? Tea?"

"Water—water would be great," she said, and Connor rushed into the small kitchen at the far side of the living room to pour her a glass.

Cami sat down next to the woman and held her hand. It was icy cold, but then, to be fair, her own hand was too. This had been a terrifying ordeal, and she still felt a sense of disbelief that they'd got there in time.

Connor brought back the water.

"Cami, you did a good job there," he said. "That was exceptional work. And for an untrained civilian, I'm proud of your physical bravery. Well done," he said in a low voice.

She felt warmed by the compliment. It was her first genuine compliment from him. And it meant the world to her.

Fifi was safe, and the killer was caught.

At last, this case was closed, and the horror was over.

EPILOGUE

It was two days later, and Cami was sitting at the student café at MIT, laptop open, waiting for a friend to join her for coffee and cake before they did an intensive study session together.

She appreciated the familiar bustle of the university environment all the more after having been jerked so far out of her comfort zone. She felt a massive sense of relief that this case was behind her, and her life was back to normal—or as close as it could get—again.

But things were not wrapped up as neatly as she'd hoped they would be.

She'd never found out what Fraser had wanted to speak to her about—that "something else" he'd mentioned. He'd been traveling nonstop, and although she'd received a short message congratulating her on the case, he hadn't mentioned it.

Cami didn't think he'd forgotten about it though. It was still hanging over her, causing a sliver of dread to ice her stomach whenever she remembered it. He might just have been too busy to investigate it before calling her in. She needed to be ready for the worst.

Her phone beeped, and she quickly turned to it, expecting it to be her friend saying she was on her way.

But it wasn't. It was Ethan texting her, and her face broke into a smile as she read the message.

"I've got a free weekend coming up. Do you have a gap? You want to go for coffee? Drinks?"

The spark she'd felt between them was mutual. Ethan liked her, and this could go further. She felt the chill in her stomach replaced by a pleasant twist of warmth as she thought about their next meeting. She was looking forward to it.

Ethan was a good guy, with charisma and confidence. He was perceptive. And he was super-smart. It was strange how chatting to him and hearing about the cases he'd handled since he'd come on board was giving her a new picture of the FBI—one that was very different from the one she'd carried in her mind, with anger and resentment, for years.

Beaming with delight, Cami texted back at once. *"Sounds great! I'm free Saturday."*

This was a date, she guessed. At least, she thought so. A date with Ethan. It had been a long time since she'd been on a date, and she was looking forward to it.

And then, she saw a message had popped up on her browser while she'd been texting him.

It was Amo-1, her hacking friend, messaging on the dark web.

Quickly, turning her screen so Cami was sure it was private, she logged into the anonymous and encrypted conversation.

"Hey Cami!"

"Hey Amo-1, what's up?"

"Listen, I was thinking about your problem. That file."

Cami's eyebrows raised. This was interesting.

"What about it?" she messaged.

"I think I might have found a fix for the program doing the corrupting."

"Seriously? That's amazing. What is it?"

"Something that will override it. There's a patch I spotted on open source today that I think would work, with a bit of tweaking. If you're interested, I'll send you the link."

"Really? It can unravel all that?"

"Well, not exactly."

Frowning, Cami interrogated her friend.

"What do you mean?"

"I mean, you'll need to go back to the original. You'll need to try and retrieve it again. And then when the malware they put into it starts activating, you run this."

Cami stared at the words, feeling conflicted, but impossibly tempted.

"I don't know if I can," she said aloud, unsure if it was really right to take this kind of risk. "I don't know if I should."

Going back into the FBI archives would expose her all over again. There was most definitely a malevolent entity who was trying to track her online movements in the archives. She didn't know if she'd gotten away with it once. This was going to be a huge additional risk.

Going back in would mean more than exposing herself to possible trouble from Fraser—which was bad and serious enough on its own. It would mean that she was basically issuing a challenge to whoever this person was. Throwing down the gauntlet.

Cami had absolutely no doubt that this would be seen as an act of deliberate aggression.

She'd be making an enemy, and she wouldn't even know who that enemy was.

But on the other hand, why were people doing such dirty work in the archives, seeding files with malware, leaving trace programs on archive records? Whoever was doing this, shouldn't be. They were as much in the wrong as she was.

And if this exposed them, then so be it. She'd have to handle the fallout if it happened.

Cami gave a decisive nod. It was worth it to find out what had happened with Jenna's investigation. And it was worth it to find out who this person was. No matter where this led her.

"Send the link," she messaged back.

JUST RIGHT
(A Cami Lark Mystery—Book 3)

With her tattoos and piercings, MIT tech genius Cami Lark is rebellious and anti-authoritarian—and finds herself in deep trouble when she hacks the FBI. Faced with the choice of prison or aiding the BAU hunt down serial killers, Cami reluctantly partners. Yet when victims of a new serial killer turn up, clearly targeted via some form of technology Cami has yet to decipher, Cami wonders if she has lost her touch. And if she doesn't solve the riddle quickly, another life may just be at stake.

"A masterpiece of thriller and mystery."
—Books and Movie Reviews, Roberto Mattos (re Once Gone)

JUST RIGHT (A Cami Lark FBI Suspense Thriller—Book 3) is the third novel in a new series by #1 bestseller and USA Today bestselling author Blake Pierce, whose bestseller Once Gone (a free download) has received over 7,000 five star ratings and reviews.

In his twisted game of cat and mouse, the killer keeps Cami guessing until the very end.

A page-turning and harrowing crime thriller featuring a brilliant and tortured FBI agent, the CAMI LARK series is a riveting mystery, packed with non-stop action, suspense, twists and turns, revelations, and driven by a breakneck pace that will keep you flipping pages late into the night. Fans of Rachel Caine, Teresa Driscoll and Robert Dugoni are sure to fall in love.

Books #4 and #5 in the series—JUST FORGET and JUST ONCE—are also available.

"An edge of your seat thriller in a new series that keeps you turning pages! ...So many twists, turns and red herrings… I can't wait to see what happens next."
—Reader review (Her Last Wish)

"A strong, complex story about two FBI agents trying to stop a serial killer. If you want an author to capture your attention and have you guessing, yet trying to put the pieces together, Pierce is your author!"
—Reader review (Her Last Wish)

"A typical Blake Pierce twisting, turning, roller coaster ride suspense thriller. Will have you turning the pages to the last sentence of the last chapter!!!"
—Reader review (City of Prey)

"Right from the start we have an unusual protagonist that I haven't seen done in this genre before. The action is nonstop… A very atmospheric novel that will keep you turning pages well into the wee hours."
—Reader review (City of Prey)

"Everything that I look for in a book… a great plot, interesting characters, and grabs your interest right away. The book moves along at a breakneck pace and stays that way until the end. Now on go I to book two!"
—Reader review (Girl, Alone)

"Exciting, heart pounding, edge of your seat book… a must read for mystery and suspense readers!"
—Reader review (Girl, Alone)

Blake Pierce

Blake Pierce is the USA Today bestselling author of the RILEY PAGE mystery series, which includes seventeen books. Blake Pierce is also the author of the MACKENZIE WHITE mystery series, comprising fourteen books; of the AVERY BLACK mystery series, comprising six books; of the KERI LOCKE mystery series, comprising five books; of the MAKING OF RILEY PAIGE mystery series, comprising six books; of the KATE WISE mystery series, comprising seven books; of the CHLOE FINE psychological suspense mystery, comprising six books; of the JESSIE HUNT psychological suspense thriller series, comprising twenty six books; of the AU PAIR psychological suspense thriller series, comprising three books; of the ZOE PRIME mystery series, comprising six books; of the ADELE SHARP mystery series, comprising sixteen books, of the EUROPEAN VOYAGE cozy mystery series, comprising six books; of the LAURA FROST FBI suspense thriller, comprising eleven books; of the ELLA DARK FBI suspense thriller, comprising fourteen books (and counting); of the A YEAR IN EUROPE cozy mystery series, comprising nine books, of the AVA GOLD mystery series, comprising six books; of the RACHEL GIFT mystery series, comprising ten books (and counting); of the VALERIE LAW mystery series, comprising nine books (and counting); of the PAIGE KING mystery series, comprising eight books (and counting); of the MAY MOORE mystery series, comprising eleven books (and counting); the CORA SHIELDS mystery series, comprising five books (and counting); of the NICKY LYONS mystery series, comprising seven books (and counting), of the CAMI LARK mystery series, comprising five books (and counting), and of the new AMBER YOUNG mystery series, comprising five books (and counting).

An avid reader and lifelong fan of the mystery and thriller genres, Blake loves to hear from you, so please feel free to visit www.blakepierceauthor.com to learn more and stay in touch.

BOOKS BY BLAKE PIERCE

AMBER YOUNG MYSTERY SERIES
ABSENT PITY (Book #1)
ABSENT REMORSE (Book #2)
ABSENT FEELING (Book #3)
ABSENT MERCY (Book #4)
ABSENT REASON (Book #5)

CAMI LARK MYSTERY SERIES
JUST ME (Book #1)
JUST OUTSIDE (Book #2)
JUST RIGHT (Book #3)
JUST FORGET (Book #4)
JUST ONCE (Book #5)

NICKY LYONS MYSTERY SERIES
ALL MINE (Book #1)
ALL HIS (Book #2)
ALL HE SEES (Book #3)
ALL ALONE (Book #4)
ALL FOR ONE (Book #5)
ALL HE TAKES (Book #6)
ALL FOR ME (Book #7)

CORA SHIELDS MYSTERY SERIES
UNDONE (Book #1)
UNWANTED (Book #2)
UNHINGED (Book #3)
UNSAID (Book #4)
UNGLUED (Book #5)

MAY MOORE SUSPENSE THRILLER
NEVER RUN (Book #1)
NEVER TELL (Book #2)
NEVER LIVE (Book #3)
NEVER HIDE (Book #4)

NEVER FORGIVE (Book #5)
NEVER AGAIN (Book #6)
NEVER LOOK BACK (Book #7)
NEVER FORGET (Book #8)
NEVER LET GO (Book #9)
NEVER PRETEND (Book #10)
NEVER HESITATE (Book #11)

PAIGE KING MYSTERY SERIES
THE GIRL HE PINED (Book #1)
THE GIRL HE CHOSE (Book #2)
THE GIRL HE TOOK (Book #3)
THE GIRL HE WISHED (Book #4)
THE GIRL HE CROWNED (Book #5)
THE GIRL HE WATCHED (Book #6)
THE GIRL HE WANTED (Book #7)
THE GIRL HE CLAIMED (Book #8)

VALERIE LAW MYSTERY SERIES
NO MERCY (Book #1)
NO PITY (Book #2)
NO FEAR (Book #3)
NO SLEEP (Book #4)
NO QUARTER (Book #5)
NO CHANCE (Book #6)
NO REFUGE (Book #7)
NO GRACE (Book #8)
NO ESCAPE (Book #9)

RACHEL GIFT MYSTERY SERIES
HER LAST WISH (Book #1)
HER LAST CHANCE (Book #2)
HER LAST HOPE (Book #3)
HER LAST FEAR (Book #4)
HER LAST CHOICE (Book #5)
HER LAST BREATH (Book #6)
HER LAST MISTAKE (Book #7)
HER LAST DESIRE (Book #8)
HER LAST REGRET (Book #9)
HER LAST HOUR (Book #10)

AVA GOLD MYSTERY SERIES
CITY OF PREY (Book #1)
CITY OF FEAR (Book #2)
CITY OF BONES (Book #3)
CITY OF GHOSTS (Book #4)
CITY OF DEATH (Book #5)
CITY OF VICE (Book #6)

A YEAR IN EUROPE
A MURDER IN PARIS (Book #1)
DEATH IN FLORENCE (Book #2)
VENGEANCE IN VIENNA (Book #3)
A FATALITY IN SPAIN (Book #4)

ELLA DARK FBI SUSPENSE THRILLER
GIRL, ALONE (Book #1)
GIRL, TAKEN (Book #2)
GIRL, HUNTED (Book #3)
GIRL, SILENCED (Book #4)
GIRL, VANISHED (Book 5)
GIRL ERASED (Book #6)
GIRL, FORSAKEN (Book #7)
GIRL, TRAPPED (Book #8)
GIRL, EXPENDABLE (Book #9)
GIRL, ESCAPED (Book #10)
GIRL, HIS (Book #11)
GIRL, LURED (Book #12)
GIRL, MISSING (Book #13)
GIRL, UNKNOWN (Book #14)

LAURA FROST FBI SUSPENSE THRILLER
ALREADY GONE (Book #1)
ALREADY SEEN (Book #2)
ALREADY TRAPPED (Book #3)
ALREADY MISSING (Book #4)
ALREADY DEAD (Book #5)
ALREADY TAKEN (Book #6)
ALREADY CHOSEN (Book #7)
ALREADY LOST (Book #8)

ALREADY HIS (Book #9)
ALREADY LURED (Book #10)
ALREADY COLD (Book #11)

EUROPEAN VOYAGE COZY MYSTERY SERIES
MURDER (AND BAKLAVA) (Book #1)
DEATH (AND APPLE STRUDEL) (Book #2)
CRIME (AND LAGER) (Book #3)
MISFORTUNE (AND GOUDA) (Book #4)
CALAMITY (AND A DANISH) (Book #5)
MAYHEM (AND HERRING) (Book #6)

ADELE SHARP MYSTERY SERIES
LEFT TO DIE (Book #1)
LEFT TO RUN (Book #2)
LEFT TO HIDE (Book #3)
LEFT TO KILL (Book #4)
LEFT TO MURDER (Book #5)
LEFT TO ENVY (Book #6)
LEFT TO LAPSE (Book #7)
LEFT TO VANISH (Book #8)
LEFT TO HUNT (Book #9)
LEFT TO FEAR (Book #10)
LEFT TO PREY (Book #11)
LEFT TO LURE (Book #12)
LEFT TO CRAVE (Book #13)
LEFT TO LOATHE (Book #14)
LEFT TO HARM (Book #15)
LEFT TO RUIN (Book #16)

THE AU PAIR SERIES
ALMOST GONE (Book#1)
ALMOST LOST (Book #2)
ALMOST DEAD (Book #3)

ZOE PRIME MYSTERY SERIES
FACE OF DEATH (Book#1)
FACE OF MURDER (Book #2)
FACE OF FEAR (Book #3)
FACE OF MADNESS (Book #4)

FACE OF FURY (Book #5)
FACE OF DARKNESS (Book #6)

A JESSIE HUNT PSYCHOLOGICAL SUSPENSE SERIES

THE PERFECT WIFE (Book #1)
THE PERFECT BLOCK (Book #2)
THE PERFECT HOUSE (Book #3)
THE PERFECT SMILE (Book #4)
THE PERFECT LIE (Book #5)
THE PERFECT LOOK (Book #6)
THE PERFECT AFFAIR (Book #7)
THE PERFECT ALIBI (Book #8)
THE PERFECT NEIGHBOR (Book #9)
THE PERFECT DISGUISE (Book #10)
THE PERFECT SECRET (Book #11)
THE PERFECT FAÇADE (Book #12)
THE PERFECT IMPRESSION (Book #13)
THE PERFECT DECEIT (Book #14)
THE PERFECT MISTRESS (Book #15)
THE PERFECT IMAGE (Book #16)
THE PERFECT VEIL (Book #17)
THE PERFECT INDISCRETION (Book #18)
THE PERFECT RUMOR (Book #19)
THE PERFECT COUPLE (Book #20)
THE PERFECT MURDER (Book #21)
THE PERFECT HUSBAND (Book #22)
THE PERFECT SCANDAL (Book #23)
THE PERFECT MASK (Book #24)
THE PERFECT RUSE (Book #25)
THE PERFECT VENEER (Book #26)

CHLOE FINE PSYCHOLOGICAL SUSPENSE SERIES

NEXT DOOR (Book #1)
A NEIGHBOR'S LIE (Book #2)
CUL DE SAC (Book #3)
SILENT NEIGHBOR (Book #4)
HOMECOMING (Book #5)
TINTED WINDOWS (Book #6)

KATE WISE MYSTERY SERIES

IF SHE KNEW (Book #1)
IF SHE SAW (Book #2)
IF SHE RAN (Book #3)
IF SHE HID (Book #4)
IF SHE FLED (Book #5)
IF SHE FEARED (Book #6)
IF SHE HEARD (Book #7)

THE MAKING OF RILEY PAIGE SERIES
WATCHING (Book #1)
WAITING (Book #2)
LURING (Book #3)
TAKING (Book #4)
STALKING (Book #5)
KILLING (Book #6)

RILEY PAIGE MYSTERY SERIES
ONCE GONE (Book #1)
ONCE TAKEN (Book #2)
ONCE CRAVED (Book #3)
ONCE LURED (Book #4)
ONCE HUNTED (Book #5)
ONCE PINED (Book #6)
ONCE FORSAKEN (Book #7)
ONCE COLD (Book #8)
ONCE STALKED (Book #9)
ONCE LOST (Book #10)
ONCE BURIED (Book #11)
ONCE BOUND (Book #12)
ONCE TRAPPED (Book #13)
ONCE DORMANT (Book #14)
ONCE SHUNNED (Book #15)
ONCE MISSED (Book #16)
ONCE CHOSEN (Book #17)

MACKENZIE WHITE MYSTERY SERIES
BEFORE HE KILLS (Book #1)
BEFORE HE SEES (Book #2)
BEFORE HE COVETS (Book #3)
BEFORE HE TAKES (Book #4)

BEFORE HE NEEDS (Book #5)
BEFORE HE FEELS (Book #6)
BEFORE HE SINS (Book #7)
BEFORE HE HUNTS (Book #8)
BEFORE HE PREYS (Book #9)
BEFORE HE LONGS (Book #10)
BEFORE HE LAPSES (Book #11)
BEFORE HE ENVIES (Book #12)
BEFORE HE STALKS (Book #13)
BEFORE HE HARMS (Book #14)

AVERY BLACK MYSTERY SERIES
CAUSE TO KILL (Book #1)
CAUSE TO RUN (Book #2)
CAUSE TO HIDE (Book #3)
CAUSE TO FEAR (Book #4)
CAUSE TO SAVE (Book #5)
CAUSE TO DREAD (Book #6)

KERI LOCKE MYSTERY SERIES
A TRACE OF DEATH (Book #1)
A TRACE OF MURDER (Book #2)
A TRACE OF VICE (Book #3)
A TRACE OF CRIME (Book #4)
A TRACE OF HOPE (Book #5)

Made in United States
Orlando, FL
11 July 2023

34965061R10102